Vaila's Capri

Helen Ross

HELEN ROSS was born in Edinburgh, in 1921. Although Scottish by birth, she spent most of her early childhood in the windswept Shetland Islands — "The Land of the Midnight Sun" — far from the North of Scotland, just south of the Arctic Circle. Helen's heart has always been in the Shetlands, and she still has relatives living on Shetland's most northerly island, Unst.

Helen was married to her beloved Archie for 66 years, and they had two sons, Irvine and William. Helen and Archie travelled extensively, Africa and the Isle of Capri being two of her favourite destinations.

Helen's interest in story writing started when she, Archie and their family moved to Australia in the early 1960s. Now in her 80s, Helen is publishing her first novel, which reflects much of her travel experience as well as her keen love of history.

Helen now lives on the New South Wales Central Coast with her faithful dog, Kirsty.

Published in Australia by Sid Harta Publishers Pty Ltd,
ABN: 46 119 415 842
23 Stirling Crescent, Glen Waverley, Victoria 3150 Australia
Telephone: +61 3 9560 9920, Facsimile: +61 3 9545 1742
E-mail: author@sidharta.com.au

First published in Australia 2010
This edition published 2010
Copyright © Helen Ross 2010
Cover design, typesetting: Chameleon Print Design

The right of Helen Ross to be identified as the Author of the Work has been asserted in accordance with the Copyright, Designs and Patents Act 1988.

Ross, Helen
Vaila's Capri
ISBN: 1-921642-98-X   EAN13: 978-1-921642-98-2
pp138

This book is dedicated to my beloved husband of 66 years, Archie, who encouraged me at all times to put pen to paper to share with others, the interest and excitement of our travels together.

Jany. 2013,

To John,
A pleasure to know.

Kindest regards.

Helen Ross.

Characters

Joseph	Servant at Mount Nelson Hotel, Cape Town
Luigi	Tony's friend; husband of Theresa
Magnus	May's brother
Mara	A local Capresian girl
Margherita	Wife of Tony's cousin, Atteo, from Naples
Maria	Cook to Tony's parents
Mario	One of Tony's friends
May	Vaila's friend
Michael Rennie	Film actor
Miro	Head Chef and son of owner of Mount Nelson Hotel, Cape Town
Nan	An American tourist
Nicolena	The village storyteller
Olaf	Vaila's university tutor
Phyllis Calvert	Film actor
Robert	Vaila's fellow travelling companion
Rosina	Tony's and Vaila's housekeeper
Rosinella	The fishmonger
Saveria	Sister to Miro; wife of Dario
Theresa	Tony's friend; wife of Luigi
Vaila	Born on the Island of Vaila in the Shetland Isles; wife of Captain De Marco (Tony)
Zia Mara	Wife of Zio Carlo
Zio Carlo	Old family friend of Tony's parents; owner of Mount Nelson Hotel, Cape Town; husband of Zia Mara; father of Miro and Saveria

Chapter 1

A COOL BREEZE, carrying the scent of heather and herrings and Aberdeen's wet pavements, ruffled Vaila's hair as she stood with her hands gripping the rail of the Italian ship, the *SS Capri*, the cargo vessel that was to take her to Africa.

Beside her, a fellow student, Elizabeth, drew closer as the ship left the wharf. Oblivious to the appreciative glance that fell on her from the eyes of a passing steward, Vaila pushed her mop of unruly golden hair back from her forehead.

The ship's siren screeched, coloured streamers snapped. On the receding wharf, now seemingly tinier by the growing distance, Vaila's mother and father stood and waved. Her friends, May and James, jumped up and down wildly.

"Sorry to say goodbye?" asked Elizabeth, as the cheering began to fade.

Vaila's eyes were moist as she confessed, "I wa'd be," in her soft Shetland brogue, "but, oh Africa! Is it na'e exciting?" As the figures gradually disappeared from sight Vaila's thoughts turned back to her island home, after which she had been named. What a wonderful childhood she had enjoyed. Although an only child she had never felt lonely. May and her brother, Magnus, had always been there. Even when boarding at the high school in Aberdeen, May and she had shared a room. Only when university level was reached had their ways parted. Vaila wanted to study archaeology at Aberdeen University. She had an unquenchable thirst for knowledge and her dream had always been to travel to other countries to experience the different cultures for herself. May's ambition was to be a nurse, while Magnus wanted to study agriculture at the college in Orkney.

Vaila's dreaming about the past was interrupted by Elizabeth, who was her friend of three years. They had both studied the same subject at university. "My word, your boyfriend, James, is so handsome; I don't know if I'd be leaving him for so long."

Vaila laughed, thinking, 'Dear old James, I wish I could return the affection he so justly deserves.' "Yes, Elizabeth," she answered, "He's a super person. We have been friends for a long time. We met when he came to my home on business. He is a buyer for his father's knitwear firm in Aberdeen. Shetland knitwear is renowned for its intricate patterns and the soft quality of the wool. My mother has been a designer, successful in reviving the old Shetland crafts, and encouraging the local women to knit modern garments."

"I guess you'll never leave your beloved namesake island, Vaila," said Elizabeth, also thinking at the same time that her friend was totally unaware of how stunning she looked. Her golden hair was supposedly swept up in a topknot, but still some curls escaped in the stiff North Sea breeze. Her outfit did credit to Shetland knitting. The ensemble was knitted in two-ply island wool. The top was in white with a yoke of pale and dark blue Nordic design knitted into the neck and sleeves. The skirt was in a dark blue, lined with taffeta that gave a gentle rustle as she walked.

Vaila replied, "I suppose I could marry Magnus and stay on the island for evermore, or even James, at least Aberdeen isn't too far away. Perhaps I am in love with one of them and don't know it. But when I marry, it must be for love, just like my own parents."

The last outline Vaila could make out was of her father, tall and distinguished. He was a well-known ornithologist and would be keen to return to the Shetland Islands where many students came from the mainland to study the rare Snowy Owl. This bird had only been found in the last few years, nesting in a small island called Uyea. Vaila's life had always been full of interest; meeting people from many countries, as both her parents were top in their professions, her father in ornithology and her mother a designer.

Vaila's father was unsure of passenger cargo ships,

but that morning when they all boarded the *SS Capri* he had been agreeably surprised. At first he had disapproved of the five budding archaeologists making the trip to Rhodesia, despite knowing their tutor, Olaf. If it were possible, they had all decided to travel by sea to Cape Town and were delighted to discover that the *SS Capri* was calling at Aberdeen for cargo. The agent had managed to book six berths for them, and Vaila's father, in the face of the exuberance shown by Vaila, had relented, and joined in with his usual zest for life.

Vaila anxiously scanned the horizon but Aberdeen had disappeared. Their fellow companions, Hamish, Robert and John, were already deep in conversation around the bar, no doubt discussing their forthcoming adventure. "Let's take a stroll around the ship, Elizabeth," said Vaila, as already a North Sea breeze was coming up.

"Isn't the Captain absolutely divine?" asked Elizabeth. "I almost swooned at the sight of him. He had eyes for none but you, Vaila."

"Nonsense," replied Vaila, "he was too busy seeing to the ship. Aberdeen is a tricky harbour to get out of. You landlubbers haven't a clue about the sea."

"Let's get freshened up for lunch," said Elizabeth. "I bet the boys will get off their mark at the thought of food. I have a lovely posy of flowers in my cabin with no card attached. I wonder who sent it."

"So do I," said Vaila. "It must have been the head steward. I guess he was trying to make us feel at home. Oh, here he comes now. Let's thank him."

The steward, Bernardo, shook his head when Vaila thanked him, and said in his delightful Italian accent, "Captain's orders for the ladies, miss. Lunch will be served at 1 o'clock in the dining room."

The girls went to their respective cabins and as Vaila entered hers she remembered the little parcel that James had pressed into her hand as he left the ship. What could it be?

She knew the other parcels contained her favourite cake, biscuits and Shetland cheese, all made by the ever-faithful Aggie, who had been housekeeper to her parents for many years. Aggie had been horrified at the thought of Vaila going to darkest Africa, a land so far away and full of mystery. She had looked on this expedition with grave suspicion. Vaila's going to boarding school in Aberdeen had been traumatic for Aggie as she felt mainland people were so different. But Africa! That, in her opinion, was a heathen land.

Vaila opened the parcel from James. There, nestling in a blue velvet box, lay an exquisite bracelet. Attached was a card that read, 'With all my love, James.' The bracelet was worked in silver with a Nordic design. Vaila slipped it on her wrist. The design had been copied so faithfully from a Viking treasure that May and she had discovered on one of the remote islands near her own birthplace of Vaila.

James had worked hard to interest the local silversmith in Lerwick to copy these works of art. It had become a thriving industry in the Shetlands and the treasure now lay in the Museum of Antiquities in Edinburgh. James and Vaila hoped it would be returned to the Shetland Islands when a new museum was built.

The ship gave a lurch. 'Feels like a heavy sea coming up,' thought Vaila. Used to rough passages between Lerwick and Aberdeen for most of her life, she still loved the sea in all its moods. At the moment, the waves seemed to reach a crescendo, and then die away with a sigh of relief. She began imagining how the sea would be pounding the shores of her island. She gave herself a shake, thinking, 'This is no time to be homesick.'

At that moment Elizabeth appeared at the cabin doorway, saying, "Oh Vaila, I feel terrible. What's happening?"

Chapter 2

Vaila was concerned, as Elizabeth was not used to sea travel. Living in Aberdeen, an occasional jaunt on a small boat in relatively calm water would be the extent of her sea travel.

Vaila saw how pale her friend looked. "I think you're a bit seasick, Elizabeth. Best if you lie down for a while now, and later on you may feel like getting some fresh air. Perhaps we will have a walk along the deck later in the afternoon. I'll bring you some dry cracker biscuits; they are excellent for any squeamishness." All this was said in a bright voice as she helped Elizabeth to her cabin and coaxed her to lie down.

Poor Elizabeth by this time felt very seasick. The ship was on a heavy roll. Her reply was not very encouraging, sounding more like a groan to Vaila.

"See you later, I will help you to unpack, so don't worry," she said, closing the door.

Vaila entered the dining room and was impressed with the interior decorating, done in pale blue and white, with paintings of ships on the walls. The boys and Olaf stood up as she entered, enquiring as to the whereabouts of Elizabeth, and were concerned to hear of her seasickness.

A figure appeared in the doorway as Vaila sat down. She was absolutely mesmerised. There stood the Captain, a tall man dressed in his uniform that emphasised his broad shoulders and his striking appearance. His deep brown eyes beneath strong, dark brows swept over them and the hint of a smile touched the angular lines of his mouth as he noted the vacant chair. "Is your friend sick, Miss Vaila? Don't worry, we'll look after her," he said.

The brilliance of his gaze sent shivers down Vaila's spine and continued as he spoke. "We're so glad to have you on board. Unfortunately, I cannot join you for lunch but will look forward to meeting you all at dinner tonight."

With that he gave a slight bow and walked out. Vaila trembled; the sound of his voice had a magnetic effect on her. Never in her whole life had another human being had such a power over her.

"Well," said Hamish, "that is the famous Captain De Marco. I believe your father, Vaila, was most impressed with his knowledge of local matters."

Vaila felt her cheeks burning as she thought of the Captain. The conversation was jolly, but Hamish seemed over-anxious about Elizabeth. 'Could there be a romance here?' wondered Vaila. Somehow she had never suspected anything other than friendship between them. The conversation turned to what they would do each day. Olaf decided to set aside four hours to study. Already the group was well versed on the inhabitants of Rhodesia: Matabele warriors and the Shonas. How they lived could be traced back through their excavations. Hamish was interested in pottery, and was adamant that a way of life could be traced back through their clay utensils.

"I must go and see Elizabeth," said Vaila. "Please excuse me." On entering the cabin she found Elizabeth still looking pretty seasick. A tray had been placed beside her bed complete with a napkin, a plate of dry biscuits and a bottle of soda water. "Quite a feast you've got there," said Vaila. "At least you've tried to eat part of a biscuit." The boys had written a humorous card for Elizabeth, *'Oh, for a life on the ocean wave, and there she was, lying on the crest of a big wave'*. Elizabeth gave a giggle as Vaila read it. "Thank goodness you can laugh, Elizabeth," said Vaila. "Dinner's at seven," and then continued to give her a run down on the luncheon conversation.

Elizabeth accepted Vaila's offer to unpack for her. Vaila opened the case and found a picture of Hamish on top. "Just put that photograph in the drawer," said Elizabeth, who was trying to cover her embarrassment with a hurried remark about her farewell gifts of note-paper, pens and, of all things, a sun helmet.

"Doctor Livingstone, I presume," said Vaila, as she put it on her head. Even Elizabeth, despite her feeling sick, could not help but smile. Both girls gave way to laughter.

"I must go," said Vaila. "I'll pop in later and see how you are. I may just borrow that hat some time," was her parting remark as she closed the door behind her.

As she entered her cabin Vaila decided to unpack her case, thinking at the same time, 'Thank goodness Elizabeth didn't enquire about Captain De Marco,' because she may have given herself away. Even the mention of his name caused her cheeks to burn.

She put aside Aggie's two parcels of food, and then read her Bon Voyage card. The words took on a special meaning as she read:

Think deeply, speak gently, love much, laugh often,
Work hard, give freely, pay promptly, pray earnestly,
and be kind to everyone.
Follow these words carefully and this world will be a
much better place in which to live.

Aggie was such a practical person, almost uncanny at times with her premonitions about the future.

As Vaila hung up her clothes she thought, 'What shall I wear tonight?' Normally she was not a fussy person, but tonight was special. She wanted to look her best for

Captain De Marco. The ship was still heaving. 'Poor Elizabeth,' she thought, 'the sea will have to calm down a bit before she gets her sea legs.'

Time passed quickly. Vaila decided to wear her favourite cornflower blue dress. The white collar was wide and deep with a pattern of seashells and waves. With her swept-up hairstyle she wore silver shell earrings that matched the bracelet James had given her. White sandals and a bag completed her attire.

Her skin required very little make-up, just a dusting of powder along with a pink lipstick that complemented her deep blue eyes. Unaware of how stunning she looked, Vaila hurriedly patted her hair once more, and then the dinner bell sounded, so she quickly shut the cabin door and popped in to see her friend.

Elizabeth was sitting up in bed with a daintily set dinner tray in front of her. "I might try a little soup," said Elizabeth, looking up at Vaila. "Gosh you look super in that dress."

Vaila laughed, saying, "Thank you. Your approval means a lot to me. I'm glad to see you looking better. I must be off now."

The menfolk were having pre-dinner drinks when she entered the dining room. Captain De Marco came forward saying, "Good evening, Vaila," and kissed her hand. The gesture was so natural and obviously a custom of his country, but so very foreign to Vaila's way of life.

Vaila saw the admiration in his eyes and to her dismay, felt a deep flush spread to her cheeks as he said, "Would you like a sherry? Dry or sweet, Vaila?"

Vaila stuttered, "D-d-dry please."

He signalled to the steward who gave Vaila her glass of sherry, while the Captain went on to say that he had some Italian wines for dinner and had just been telling her friends about the wine list.

Vaila managed to say in a normal voice, "Please thank the steward for looking after Elizabeth, her dinner tray looked most appetising. This sherry is very nice." At that moment the boys came over. Hamish was anxious to hear about Elizabeth.

Dinner was a great success and the conversation flowed freely. Vaila loved the red wine that was grown by a member of the De Marco family who lived near Naples.

With relief Vaila learned that the Captain was not married and still lived with his parents on the Isle of Capri. Although his father was over eighty he still took an active interest in the shipping business.

The food was beautifully presented and cooked. The china was embossed with the crest of the shipping line, a tiny green island surrounded by the deep blue sea.

The ship's name, *SS Capri*, was embossed in gold

lettering. On the fine white china it looked superb. All this intrigued Vaila, even the little coffee cups carried the same design.

During the conversation, the Captain asked them to call him Tony, when they met socially. Seemingly, he had trained in Italy, and then finished his Navigation and Second Mate's Certificates at Leith Nautical College, Edinburgh. "Now you know where my Scottish accent comes from," the Captain said laughingly. "Scotland is a beautiful country, but the weather is very changeable." With his accent and comments about the weather, the Captain drew chuckles from his guests.

Turning to Vaila he said, "You must tell us more about this island of yours. It does sound different. I, too, live on an island, in the Bay of Naples, it's called Capri, and hence the ship and crest bears the name of my birthplace."

Vaila could hear the sentiment in his voice as he told them that the island had two levels and his family had always lived on the upper part. Vaila warmed at the thought of someone with the same feelings for their homeland as herself.

"Of course, I will tell you all about my island of Vaila." Her reply was spontaneous, as she showed delight at his words.

Hearing this, Hamish, Robert and John, gave a shout. Being from the mainland of Scotland they could not understand the feeling of possessiveness that Vaila had about this remote island, so far north from the mainland. "Oh, no," they chorused, "now we have two of them."

Arrangements were made for a tour of the ship when the weather was more stable. "Don't forget, lifeboat drill is essential," said Captain De Marco. "We assemble on the upper deck at ten in the morning. Lifejackets must be worn, and this ensures that you know where they are kept in your cabins and how to put them on.

The sea was still very rough and the Captain excused himself, saying, "Please forgive me, I must go up to the bridge and see that everything is in order. Help yourself to more coffee and liqueurs." He gave Vaila a deep, penetrating look that, to her mind, said everything.

In her cabin that night Vaila went over the evening in her mind. She was now sure of her attraction to Captain De Marco.

'He probably has lots of girlfriends,' she thought, 'but I do like him.' Even as she fell asleep she could feel the warmth of his kiss on her hand.

Next morning, there was a stiff breeze blowing. A knock on Vaila's door promptly at seven, announced the arrival of tea and toast. Bernardo said, "It's a nice morning, miss," as he placed the tray at her bedside. "Best to close your porthole as we could have some rain and it may blow in. Breakfast is at eight-thirty and lifeboat drill at 10 am." His flashing smile made the day ahead feel good to Vaila.

Elizabeth was much better when Vaila called along, and was up and dressed. Both girls wore trousers and safari jackets. Elizabeth's dark, curly hair and deep blue eyes were in startling contrast to Vaila's golden looks. "We must remember to lay out our lifejackets for the 10 o'clock drill," said Vaila.

"It seems a lot of fuss for nothing," said Elizabeth.

Vaila secretly applauded the fuss and bother, as she knew how treacherous the sea could be. "Better to be safe than sorry," she quoted as they made their way to the dining room. The waves of the North Atlantic Sea pounded relentlessly against the ship as they made steady progress down the coastline of Britain.

After breakfast they went to their cabins and put on their lifejackets, then made their way to the upper deck where the menfolk were all assembled. First Officer, Alberto, gave them a brief talk about what to do in an emergency, showing them the lifeboat, which was equipped with water, rations and flares. "We like to be prepared for every crisis," said Alberto, who obviously took great pride in the smooth running of the ship.

"We must remember to bring some of Vaila's food with us," quipped John in his droll Scottish accent. Everyone burst out laughing, as they had all enjoyed Vaila's food parcels while at university.

Chapter 3

A FTER A WEEK AT SEA A ROUTINE HAD BEEN ESTABLISHED. Vaila, Elizabeth, and the boys, along with their mentor, Olaf, formed a class every morning and afternoon. Having had a tour of the ship their surroundings were now familiar. Any free time they had, Hamish and Elizabeth paired off, going for long walks around the deck. They were obviously very happy in each other's company.

Vaila was still reticent to speak up in the Captain's company, so was surprised when he asked her to go for a walk one evening after dinner. He was an excellent conversationalist and she loved the way he spoke about his island home. Tony, as she now called him, gave a graphic description of the boat trip from Naples to Capri.

"Looking back at Naples from the ship is like a picture postcard. Although, I must say Naples itself is busy, people and traffic everywhere. I love to sail on the Bay of Naples and visit the islands. Pompeii is well worth a visit, so is the Blue Grotto. The perfume of oranges and lemons fill the air as you draw near to Capri. Some day you must visit my home, Vaila."

Vaila was intrigued and went on to tell him about her island home. Although there were no lush fruit or trees, the Shetland ponies, sheep and collie dogs, had all been part of her life.

"Your father is a very interesting man. He has a dark complexion," said the Captain.

Vaila went on to explain how her people had struggled for an existence on the island. Vikings had invaded the Shetlands in the early days and many streets still bore their names. Spaniards, who survived the wreck of a ship from the Armada fleet, settled there, marrying the local girls. This would account for the dark brown eyes and black hair that gave some of the Islanders such a distinctive look.

Captain De Marco listened with great interest as Vaila poured out her heart to him.

"You certainly did not inherit Spanish looks, Vaila," he interrupted, in his carefully spoken English. Already this lovely girl had captivated him completely. Her island accent became more evident as she spoke about her home.

"What about this treasure you found?" asked the Captain. He was eyeing the bracelet that Vaila wore. "Was James a great friend of yours?" Having heard the story of the gift he was anxious to learn more about her feelings for this admirer.

Much to his relief, Vaila replied, "James will always

be a friend to me. He is like one of the family." She went on to tell him that James was intrigued with the skill of the knitters as the patterns were all done from memory. Swaying trees and vines were carefully worked into the designs.

"Having no trees on your islands would make this difficult?" asked the Captain.

"Yes," replied Vaila. "This confirms the presence of Spanish sailors who must have related stories and drawn pictures of their homeland. I do love these evening strolls after dinner, Tony. We must be nearing the South Atlantic Sea. The sunsets are becoming more vivid."

"Wait till you see an Italian sunset. A bit different to your land of the midnight sun, but spectacular just the same."

Vaila stopped walking and excitedly pointed to flying fish that were jumping on their side of the ship. "Look at the colours. The evening sunset makes the fish look like gold," she said. "Africa must be a wonderful place; I can feel the warmth in the air. I can't believe we'll soon arrive in Cape Town." Her voice trailed off as she became aware of Tony's intense gaze into her eyes.

Without any warning Tony swept Vaila into his arms, saying, "Vaila, I love you, will you marry me? You do care for me, Vaila? Please say yes."

Vaila, without hesitation replied, "I love you too, Tony, I think from the first moment we met."

Tony was elated and held her even closer, saying, "My darling girl of the islands, how I will love and care for you!" Vaila felt a surge of unforgettable happiness as their lips met. This was the moment she had often dreamed about.

Their happiness was evident to everyone as they entered the lounge to have their usual nightcap. The Captain with his arm around Vaila's waist looked fondly into her eyes, as he announced, "Vaila and I are engaged and hope to marry at the end of the year."

Elizabeth rushed forward and hugged Vaila, saying, "I'm so happy for you both," and then turned to the Captain, "and here's a special hug for you too, Tony." The Captain seemed at a loss for words.

Hamish then called out, "This calls for a celebration. Let's open a bottle of champagne." Amid great cheering, they all drank to the happy couple.

Vaila felt that it would not be long before the next rejoicing would be for Hamish and Elizabeth. 'No person in the world could be as happy as I,' thought Vaila, at the same time thinking, 'Of course, my parents and Aggie will love Tony. Who wouldn't?'

"I must write to your parents, Vaila," said Tony. "We could choose an engagement ring in Cape Town. After all, Africa is famous for its diamonds." Tony went on to say that it was the custom in his country to ask the parents' permission first, before marrying.

"I just want to buy you a ring before we part in Cape Town. I realize you must finish the three-month dig in Rhodesia to complete your final year at university. The *Capri* will return to Aberdeen after this trip when I will visit your parents and, being old fashioned, ask to marry their only daughter. You will love the Isle of Capri and the Blue Grotto, Vaila," said Tony.

As Tony uttered these words Vaila suddenly realized she would be living in a foreign land away from her homeland and family. Tony seemed to sense her feelings and gathered her into his arms, saying, "Of course you'll be free to visit your beloved island whenever you want, and our home will always be open for your family and friends."

Vaila snuggled up to him saying, with a giggle, "Imagine Aggie coming to Capri, you'll have to win her over, Tony. That will not be an easy task."

Chapter 4

"WE'RE HERE, ELIZABETH. Doesn't Cape Town look beautiful? Table Mountain sure lives up to its name. It even has a tablecloth hovering above ready to be spread over the table."

"I only hope Cape Town lives up to its high reputation," laughed Elizabeth. "You're such a romantic, Vaila. One thing I'm glad of is calm seas. Land means more to me than just looking pretty. Although I must admit, latterly I have felt a lot better."

The two girls hung over the deck rail as the *SS Capri* made towards the docks. Tugboats appeared from nowhere as the ship was eased to its berth. Dark smiling faces, complete with glistening white teeth, looked up at them. They seemed delighted to see the visitors despite the fact that their work of unloading the cargo was just beginning.

Already there was an air of anticipation aboard the ship. "I haven't seen the boys around. I wonder what they're up to."

"Hamish won't be far away. I guess they'll be working out the trip to Rhodesia." Vaila stood back from the rail and stretched up her arms to the blue, cloudless sky, saying, "I can feel the warmth of the African sun already. Heavens, Elizabeth, we don't have pretty dresses to wear tonight."

"I wish we had more clothes with us," sighed Elizabeth. "Wasn't it nice of Tony's friends to invite us all to dinner this evening? I wonder if the boys will dress up."

"Never mind them, what about us? I'm choosing my ring this afternoon so in a way this will be our engagement party. Couldn't we slip away for an hour and do a bit of shopping?"

"That sounds a super idea, Vaila. You make a time and I'll meet you. After all, Tony said he always borrows his friend's car when in Cape Town. That will save a bit of time. What sort of ring do you want?"

"I'm not sure, but I'll know when I see it. Tony has arranged with the jeweller that we meet there at 2 o'clock."

The two girls went into the details of the dresses they would like and finally decided that one dress each would not affect their luggage.

An early lunch had been arranged and between the docking of the ship and arrangements for unloading the cargo an air of excitement was present around them. Vaila loved it all as at home the arrival of a ship meant newspapers, letters and the arrival of mail order shopping.

Lunch was a jolly affair and everyone was in high spirits. Tony only had a limited time with them as he had loads of paperwork to attend to.

"I've got a car for you, Olaf. You can all see the sights of Cape Town," said Tony. "I will try and get away at two sharp, Vaila."

Olaf was ecstatic, "Thanks Tony." He was joined by a chorus of approval.

Tentatively Vaila replied, "Elizabeth and I would like to shop for about an hour. Is that possible, Tony?"

"I'll arrange a meeting place with Olaf, and then we can pick up Elizabeth and deposit you both in Cape Town's biggest department store. How's that?" laughed Tony. "One proviso. No longer than one hour." This was said as he hurried out the door.

"Shopping," groaned the boys.

Tony and Vaila were shown into the private room of the most prestigious jewellery shop in Cape Town.

The owner, Johan Nuisek, was introduced to Vaila and being Dutch was interested to learn that she came from the Shetland Isles. Vaila felt at home as Dutch ships came regularly to the islands. Johan then asked her if she had anything in mind for the design of a ring.

Vaila looked at Tony for help, but he shook his head. "It's your choice, darling."

Vaila gasped as the leather cloth that covered the tray was taken off. She pointed to the ring. There it was – a blue sapphire with a diamond on each side.

"Just like the colour of your eyes, darling," said Tony.

"Well chosen, madam. This is a wonderful piece of craftsmanship. Please try it on."

It fitted perfectly. "Can I wear it now?" 'I knew my new dress must be in a shade of blue,' thought Vaila.

Back in the car, Tony said, "I do love you, Vaila, and feel you're mine, at least half, until that gold band is placed on your finger."

Elizabeth was thrilled when she saw the ring, and the boys, who had been trying the Castle beer, stood up in unison and wished them all the best.

"This calls for champagne," said Tony.

Quickly Vaila said, "Let's wait until tonight. Then we can all relax with your friends, Tony."

"We know," male voices chorused, "you want to go shopping."

Tony dropped the girls at an imposing department store. "Pick you up at 4 o'clock sharp. Remember we're due for pre-dinner drinks at six–thirty."

"Gosh, Vaila, let's make for the dresses. Look at those sandals. Prices are reasonable."

An elegant sales assistant came over as they eyed a rack of long, cotton dresses. The girls explained what they wanted and ended up with an array of items in their sizes.

Vaila fell in love with a long, white cotton dress splattered with wonderful brilliant, blue, tropical flowers. Slits on each side made for easy walking as well as showing off her long, elegant legs. Elizabeth chose an aqua dress with dark green tropical leaves. The effect was stunning.

The assistant excused herself and returned with one pair of blue sandals and another pair of pale green. "These are on sale just now. Try them on," she said.

"Mine fit perfectly," said Vaila. "How about you, Elizabeth?"

"Like a dream."

"Prices are reasonable. I've changed the rand into pounds. Let's have the sandals as well as the dresses," Vaila said impulsively. They thanked the assistant for her help and, having fifteen minutes to spare, decided to have a cool lime drink at the outside café.

Vaila kept looking at her ring, remembering Tony's words. It seemed impossible that she could be married this time next year.

"Come on, Vaila, the ring won't disappear," laughed Elizabeth. "Here comes your fiancé, dead on time."

On the way to the ship Tony pointed out the location

of his friend's house. It nestled on the lower slopes of Table Mountain. "I'm longing to show you girls off to my friends. By the size of those parcels, I guess your shopping was successful."

The dinner was an outstanding success. Tony's friends, Theresa and Luigi, were delightful, and their two young boys adored their Uncle Tony.

"You spoil the boys, Tony. You seem to know exactly what they want each time you come," said Theresa.

Vaila felt like one of the family and loved the friendly atmosphere throughout the house. Her dress was a winner. Tony whispered to her during dinner, "You get more beautiful every time I see you."

Elizabeth and Hamish had eyes only for each other. The boys were all spruced up in dress slacks and smart shirts.

Arrangements were made for returning to the ship, and Elizabeth was to go with the boys.

Having made fond farewells to their hosts, Vaila snuggled close to Tony as he drove the car. "What's that?" said Vaila, as a rodent-like creature appeared on the road, obviously dazzled by the headlights.

"That is a Rock Dassie and is endemic to this part of

the country. Can you believe that their relative is the elephant?" said Tony, as he slowed down.

"You're having me on," laughed Vaila. "Why, it looks like a plump rabbit without ears."

"Miss Archaeologist, you should understand that nature produces all kinds of wonders, including yourself. Let's get off this road, before I kiss you to death. I know a quiet spot where we'll not be disturbed."

"Are there more animals here?" Vaila said, wondering at the same time about the quiet spot that Tony had mentioned.

"Wait till you see the baboons and porcupines, as well as the rare Silver Tree. Table Mountain is home to rich fauna and flora. It's such a pity we don't have more time here."

"I didn't know you were interested in that kind of thing," said Vaila.

"We've a lifetime to discover each other, darling." Just then, Tony swung the car into the driveway of a large, rambling house.

"What a lovely setting. What's here?" Vaila exclaimed. The soft lights from within all added to the moonlight setting.

"This is the famous Mount Nelson Hotel. Friends of my father run it. As a child I spent many holidays here. Before my mother died we came to join my father when his ship was in Cape Town."

"You've passed the parking lot."

"I go in the tradesman's entrance," laughed Tony.

Before the car came to a halt, a figure dressed in white came rushing out. "Tony, how are you? I thought you would have come for dinner," said Miro.

The two men embraced, obviously good friends. Vaila loved this show of feelings. It was so different to her upbringing. Thank goodness her parents were warm and affectionate. Although the Shetland Islanders were loving in their own way, any outward show of affection was looked upon as a weakness, especially between men. Vaila vividly remembered the response she received when she used to hug Aggie.

"Away with you now. That's enough of that," Aggie would have said, although, secretly, she would have been pleased, but unable to show her feelings.

"We've come for supper instead. Miro, this is Vaila, my fiancée." Vaila was already out of the car and came forward with her hand outstretched.

"Tony, she's beautiful. You lucky hound." Miro took Vaila's hand then kissed her on each cheek. "You are now part of our family, just like Tony."

"Thank you," replied Vaila, and impulsively kissed him on the cheek.

"Come in. The night air is cool. Mother has arranged a nice supper for you; also your favourite log fire has been lit. We've a big function on but Mum and Dad will see you later."

The wide verandah and spacious hall, all tastefully furnished, impressed Vaila. From nowhere a tall, black servant appeared dressed in a long red skirt. Miro said, "Being Head Chef, I can't stay, but Joseph here will attend to you."

"Pleased to see you, Mastah Tony," said Joseph, with a smile that showed off his white teeth to perfection. "Powder room this way, Missy."

Joseph was waiting for Vaila when she came out and pointed to a door further down the hallway. "Mastah Tony in there, Missy, please come." He opened the door for Vaila and she went in.

Tony was sitting in front of a crackling log fire and jumped up, saying, "I told you about my quiet spot, darling, didn't I?"

Vaila rushed forward, "It's perfect. What a beautiful room. It's so appropriate for you, Tony, with it's dark, polished woods and that lovely comfortable chair and the settee in which you can lose yourself." She laughed and kissed Tony rapturously.

Tony pulled her down onto the settee. "We've had so little time on our own. Let's make the most of it."

Suddenly, Vaila broke away from Tony's embrace. "Tony, what if your father doesn't like me?"

Tony's face broke into an affectionate smile. "What's

brought this on? What a silly question. My father will adore you. Besides, I've got to face up to your people as well. But darling, we're right for each other. That's all that matters."

"My people are not as demonstrative as yours, Tony, but I do love the warmth and affection that your people show so readily."

"Isn't that the most important thing, darling? Your happiness?"

Vaila snuggled down beside Tony. "I do love you. My ring is just perfect. Look how it glows in this light."

"I hope that ring doesn't take first place in your love for me," laughed Tony.

Just then there was a discreet knock at the door. "This could be supper. We'd better have some more light for Joseph," said Tony, as he rose to switch on another lamp. He then opened the door and to Vaila's eyes, Joseph seemed to glide into the room pushing a tray-mobile.

"Mastah and Missy come to see you soon, Mastah Tony. Flower is for Missy," said Joseph, as he carefully pushed the tray-mobile down beside the coffee table.

"My favourite, Joseph, lobster thermidor."

Vaila piped up, "That orchid is exquisite, Joseph."

"From Mastah Miro, Missy," replied Joseph.

"We'll have to see about that, Joseph," Tony said in

a stern voice that gave way to a laugh as he thanked him.

Joseph then proceeded to open the champagne. He turned towards the door and appeared to walk effortlessly over the black, slate floor, only turning around to say, "Enjoy your supper."

"He's gorgeous," said Vaila, as Joseph quietly closed the door behind him.

"Let's have a glass of champagne, darling."

Vaila gazed lovingly at Tony as he poured the bubbly. "To us," they said in unison. They linked arms as they took a sip from each other's glass.

"Look at the night view from the window, Tony. It's spectacular. Where will we be married? I would love to come here for our honeymoon."

"I'd be happy to get married aboard the *Capri*, darling, or even in Rhodesia. My father can't travel due to a heart condition, so whichever way we decide, he won't be there."

Vaila sat down on the settee. "Oh Tony, let's get married in Capri. My mum and dad will travel anywhere to their daughter's wedding. They just love travelling."

"My father would be so happy with that. In fact, the whole island enjoys weddings and parties. Come, let's sample some of Miro's cooking and finish the champagne." They sat and ate and drank, happily chatting while looking lovingly at each other.

Vaila clipped the orchid in her hair. "The meal was delicious. You must show me how to make that coffee, Tony." The phone rang.

Tony rose to answer, saying, "Zia Mara and Zio Carlo are on their way up. You'll love them." A light knock on the door announced their arrival. Tony went forward as the door opened, crying out, "Zia Mara!"

"Tony, my bambino," was the reply from, to Vaila's eyes, a most elegant woman.

"What about me? Come and introduce me to this charming young lady," said Zio Carlo. He was a tall, distinguished man who won Vaila's heart with his warm embrace.

"You certainly picked a winner, Tony," laughed Zio Carlo.

Soon they were all chatting away. "Lunch tomorrow, Vaila?" enquired Zia Mara. "Tony's engagement is very special to us."

"I don't think so," replied Vaila. "My time is short in Cape Town. We are bound for Rhodesia." She went on to explain about the expedition to The Great Ruins of Rhodesia.

"It's very primitive around those parts. Where will you stay?" asked Zia Mara.

"Olaf, our tutor, has made all the arrangements. Our headquarters will be in Salisbury, to where we return each weekend. I believe we are travelling in a type of home on wheels. Elizabeth and I will sleep in the van while the boys are in tents close by."

"How long will you be there?" Zio Carlo enquired.

"Too long," interrupted Tony. "Here's hoping I can make a trip to Salisbury before the three months are up. By the way, we may be marrying in Capri."

"Your father will be so happy, Tony, should you do that," said an obviously delighted Zia Mara.

"We hope you can all come to our wedding!" exclaimed Vaila.

"Just try and keep us away. Now we must toast the happy couple." Zio Carlo raised his glass. "May you both be as happy as we are."

"We spent our honeymoon in Rhodesia, Vaila."

"That's interesting, Zia Mara. Tony and I would like to spend ours here if you will have us."

"Our home is your home," said Zio Carlo. "This calls for another toast."

"Tony, that was a wonderful evening," said Vaila, as the car sped towards the docks. "I felt so happy and part of the family. It's a pity we didn't see more of Miro. I'd love to meet his sister, Saveria, and her husband, Dario, in Johannesburg some day as well."

"You will. I hope Miro is going to be my best man, and Saveria is a wonderful girl."

"Look at your ship!" The *Capri* was lying at anchor, gleaming white and gold in the moonlight. Set against the inky darkness of the Cape Town sky, it was like a fairytale, thought Vaila.

"It could be your home for part of the year."

"I'd love that, and I do hope we can visit Shetland."

"It depends on the cargo, darling. Aberdeen is certain though." Tony parked the car and they walked along the dock towards the ship. Vaila laughed, "I bet Elizabeth thought this up." At the top of the gangway, gaily waving in the night breeze was a bunch of coloured balloons.

"See you in the morning, darling," said Tony, as he kissed Vaila outside her cabin door. "You have a long journey ahead tomorrow."

Vaila gave a sigh of contentment, "I only wish you were coming. I do love you, Tony." They parted reluctantly.

The next morning after breakfast, Olaf announced that the transport would be there at ten. There was much hustle and bustle as the last minute instructions were given.

The *Capri* was due to sail at nine, and Vaila felt all churned up inside at having to say goodbye to Tony. Her friends had discreetly left them together in the lounge after all the farewells were given.

"Darling, time will soon pass," said Tony. "You have worked so hard to get this degree, we can put up with you spending another three months in The Old Ruins of Rhodesia".

"Tony, I'll miss you so much." Vaila's voice trailed off.

"Same here, sweetheart. Look, I've so much to do when I visit Shetland, what with meeting your mother and father, and relatives and friends. Then there will be the wedding at my home in Capri. You'll be the same, wait and see."

Vaila interrupted, "Of course, Tony, I'm being very thoughtless. Are you sure that your father will like me?"

"Like you, darling, he will love you, the same as I do. I hope you can come for a few weeks beforehand, to see the island and meet everyone. The Capri Islanders are a warm-hearted, generous mob. Now does that satisfy you, my darling?"

"Oh Tony, I'm so happy," said Vaila, as they clung together in a passionate embrace.

"Time to go. Come on, I'll see you to your cabin so that you can pick up your luggage. We sail at nine."

"As we leave after you, Tony, I'm going to wave you off. Olaf thought that might be possible. Don't forget to give my love to Mum, Dad and Aggie," said Vaila, with a quiver in her voice as they kissed outside the cabin door.

All around Vaila and Elizabeth there was much activity pervading the docks as the ship prepared to sail. The labourers grinned broadly, their skins glistening in the morning sun. The ropes were thrown on to the deck of the *Capri*, amidst laughing and chatter. The blue skies and sunshine all added to this as the ship was slowly towed out to sea. Vaila and Elizabeth ran right to the edge of the dock waving madly and calling,

"Goodbye everyone." Vaila silently voiced, "Goodbye, my darling Tony."

Linking arms, the girls walked slowly towards their transport. Breaking the silence, Elizabeth burst out, "Aren't the docks here so different to home? What's that smell?"

"It could be tobacco from Rhodesia," said Vaila, "or perhaps the abundance of that delicious South African fruit, Naartjies."

"That's it; you've hit the nail on the head. Imagine our dockers in shorts, bare tops and nothing on their feet," said Elizabeth with a giggle.

"Sea boots and polo jerseys are the order of the day in Aberdeen and Lerwick, for most of the year anyway.

I love this casual atmosphere. The sun makes life so much simpler. The natives' dark skin and hair seem to shine," said Vaila, looking more like her old self again.

"Vaila, I know you love Tony, but you have always been surrounded by loving parents and friends. Affection has always been part of your life."

"Yes," replied Vaila, "I have been very blessed by knowing that Mum and Dad love me dearly, and as they are absolutely devoted to each other I have total security in their love.

"When I visited your home, Elizabeth, I saw a difference between our families. Having brothers and sisters to share with was fun."

"Fun be blowed. How I envied you. At least your possessions were safe."

"Anyway, Tony and I want a large family; it's lovely to really be the centre of attraction in someone's life. I felt this with Aggie, that's why we are so close. She seemed to understand."

"Come on girls, we're all ready to go," Olaf called out, as he hurried them towards the bus.

Vaila was upset at leaving Tony, but her heart had been set on seeing The Great Ruins of Rhodesia since she was a child. Tony encouraging her to finish her degree made it a lot easier. "Lucky you, Elizabeth. Having Hamish with us is a bonus."

"I know how you must feel. Here's hoping Tony manages a visit to see you."

"Depends on whether he has another cargo for Cape Town. Even then it takes time to get up to Rhodesia."

"You're quite a sea captain's wife already, Vaila," laughed Elizabeth.

Chapter 5

"YOUR RING IS SUPER, VAILA. I think it's better you wear it on a chain around your neck. Digging in The Great Ruins of Rhodesia, despite wearing gloves, can be a tricky business. Can you imagine that at one time this was a city as big as London?"

"I sure can, Elizabeth, judging by the distance that Olaf pegs out for us every day. I hope he realises that the ruins extend for over 1,800 acres. It's nice to have Hamish working nearby. These monkeys scare me at times. Already, I've lost a mirror and comb. They move so quickly. I can't put a thing down."

"Come on girls, we may find one of your midden heaps in this Valley Complex." Hamish was jubilant, as only yesterday he had found part of a glazed Persian bowl believed to date from the 13th to 14th centuries. "Did you know that The Ruins are African in origin and belong to the medieval period? I guess this bowl was part of the trade that existed between Sofala on the Southern Coast and Great Zimbabwe."

"We know also that the Queen of Sheba was supposed to have built here, but this has been proved wrong," said Vaila. "I can't believe we've been here over two weeks now." She carefully sifted the newly dug earth through a large sieve.

"I bet you're remembering our three days in Cape Town," Elizabeth said. "It was quite a whirlwind romance with Tony. It was lovely you met his friends, and the engagement dinner they gave was superb. The views from their home were quite breathtaking."

Vaila unconsciously fingered the engagement ring around her neck, as Elizabeth reminded her of the magical time spent with Tony.

It was hard to keep her mind on the job. Her mother and father were surprised at the speed of the romance when Vaila had phoned with the news.

"Your happiness is all we want, darling," were her mother's words when they had phoned from Cape Town. "We have a big surprise for you. Aggie took it all in her stride. We're so looking forward to Tony's visit when his ship reaches Aberdeen."

"Penny for your thoughts, Vaila. You've been in a dream since we left Cape Town. Come on, let's have a cup of tea. It's nearly 10 o'clock." Hamish started to open his backpack.

It was like a prearranged signal. From nowhere monkeys appeared. "Thieving little devils," shouted Hamish. "They can't wait for a titbit. Ruins everywhere and they have to pick on us."

"At least we get a bit of peace at Masvingo. Our sleeping van has strong netting over the windows and doors," laughed Elizabeth.

"We're in a native hut, so no such luck. The Shona people are intelligent and kind, but have no control over these monkeys," said Hamish. He then asked the girls to get a cup from their packs while he produced a flask of tea.

"Olaf and the boys are working in the Great Enclosure today, or is it the Hill Complex?" queried Vaila.

"The Great Enclosure. Don't you remember how John was so enthusiastic about it being the fabled capital of the Queen of Sheba? I'm sure he expects to find her treasure. All we find are these damned monkeys." Hamish said this as he took a swipe at one.

"Olaf feels that The Great Ruins are of African origin. I guess we'll have another discussion when we go to Salisbury at the weekend."

"Oh boy, I'm looking forward to that hotel, but most of all a deep hot bath. Thirty miles to Musvingo twice a day with only a pail of water over your head for a shower, is no fun. Why would they build a city in such an outlandish spot?" asked Elizabeth.

"I believe the tsetse fly is rare around these parts, and that the Royal Kings and Queens of Great Zimbabwe preferred to live here," replied Vaila.

The monkeys were jabbering away as the team

packed up their dirty cups. "It looks like we have disappointed this mob. We'll work until two. I'm going to examine that wall at the top of the hill," said Hamish.

"That sounds good. This sun is getting a bit hot for us and not a cloud to be seen in the sky. I believe in Italy you have a siesta every afternoon, which makes sense to me," said Elizabeth, looking a bit wistful.

Vaila laughed, "So I've heard. I hope you'll come for lots of holidays. Elizabeth, I'd really love you to be my bridesmaid, if you'd like to…"

Elizabeth, who had started to dig again, replied excitedly, "Of course, it will be wonderful! The Isle of Capri will be a super setting for your wedding."

"I hope my parents and Aggie, of course, will feel the same." Vaila, who had been sifting diligently, gave a shout, "Look, I've found something! What can it be?"

Elizabeth rushed forward. "It looks interesting, like some kind of a ring. It could be a Shona's ring. I think the design resembles some sort of bird. The use of animals and birds was extensive in African spiritual belief systems. It could be the Zimbabwe bird. After all, the Shonas were a great race of people. Here's a container to put it in. We must remember to label it correctly with the spot we found it." They put it carefully in the tin, and made sure they did not disturb the earth around it.

"What a find. Olaf will be so thrilled as The Ruins

have been well searched and looted for years," said Elizabeth excitedly.

"Enough talking. We'll have an interesting evening showing it to everyone and discussing it with them," said Vaila.

That night, as they all sat around the camp table, the topic was Vaila's find. Olaf was excited, and his usual magnifying glass was in use. They all wore gloves when examining the ring. "It looks authentic to me," said Olaf. "Vaila, you have made our time here well worthwhile. Lots of people spend years on the ruins and find nothing. It's yet to be established whether the ruins are African in origin. Although, it is said to be the largest single ancient structure south of the Sahara Desert. I know that you feel strongly about this subject."

Vaila eagerly replied, "I'm ninety per cent sure."

"Must be that second sight you have, Vaila," said Hamish.

"I must admit I'm impressed with the Shona people here," piped up Elizabeth.

"Well, we're not," chorused John and Robert. "Sanitation, showering - it doesn't seem possible that the Great Zimbabwe could have been created by them."

"Enough for tonight," said Olaf. "All this can be discussed at the weekend when we meet up with the archaeologists in Salisbury."

Elizabeth and Vaila lay talking about their exciting

day and, as usual, the conversation turned to Tony. "You seem so sure about your love for him, Vaila."

"Yes, I am. He is the one for me." Her voice trailed off sleepily.

Chapter 6

T WO YEARS LATER AS VAILA LOOKED AT THE SPECTACU-
LAR VIEW from Ana Capri she felt nothing but pure
happiness. Tony was a wonderful husband. She felt a
little scared at being so contented, especially when she
felt the stirring of a new life in her body.

Vaila's mind went back to the days before her mar-
riage and her honeymoon. No girl could have had such
a gentle lover.

Although she was madly in love with Tony, and
wanted to be a perfect wife to him in every way, their
first night as man and wife could have been a disaster.
Why did she burst into tears? It was hard to understand
this overwhelming emotion. Was it fear? She loved
Tony with a fierce love yet was frightened of the most
natural culmination of two people.

Tony cradled her in his arms and kissed her gently,
saying, "I love you, darling. Please don't get upset. I'm
prepared to wait for you."

They often laugh about it all now, as Vaila can
hardly believe that she could ever have been frightened of the sexual act. Tony now tells her that her

apprehension made him even more madly in love with her.

Her time in Zimbabwe had been exciting. Discovering the authentic Shona ring had proved to be the highlight of their trip.

Vaila would never forget her first sight of Tony's island home. They had received a tremendous welcome from his uncle, aunt and cousins in Naples, and her first sight of Capri was an unforgettable experience.

This loving family had gathered on the wharf to see them off. Obviously, Tony was a much-loved nephew and cousin of Zio Benedetto, Zia Rachele, Atteo and his wife, Margherita. They had showered Vaila with love and kindness.

As the Bay of Naples receded into the distance, Vaila exclaimed, "It's just like the pictures on chocolate boxes. I always imagined that the colours had been touched up, but the blue sea and sky are even more beautiful in real life."

Tony hugged her close, saying, "Everyone loves you, darling."

"All I want is your love, Tony. I still marvel at how we met aboard your ship. I can only hope that your father likes me."

"Silly girl, he will love you the same as everyone else. By the way, all the wine, olives and wooden crates are for our wedding. That's why we had to travel by ferry.

My small launch could never have taken all that stuff on board."

"What's in the crates?" queried Vaila.

"Presents, I presume, darling. You're going to have a busy time in the next few weeks, between your parents, Aggie, and the rest of the Scottish clan arriving."

Vaila was fascinated as the ferryboat made its daily run to various ports of call, but as the ship drew near the Isle of Capri, she was enraptured. The perfume of oranges and lemons wafted towards them. Set in the deep, blue sea, with a cloudless, sapphire sky above, the island took Vaila's breath away. Jagged rocks standing like sentinels in the sea seemed to guard this island paradise.

"You're very quiet, darling. Is everything all right?"

"Tony, I've the uncanny feeling that I've been here before."

"Enough of that," laughed Tony. "Isn't one Aggie in the family sufficient?"

Tony knew the crew and their good-natured banter was evident despite Vaila's limited knowledge of the language. Hands played an important part in their speech and one could almost guess what they were talking about as they gesticulated wildly.

The ferry slowed down as they drew near the jetty. Vaila was amazed to see all the people. They were waving and calling out, *"Contento Sposalizio."*

"That means 'Happy Wedding', darling," said Tony. "My people love weddings. The whole island will be there."

The view from their home was spectacular. Tony had all this in mind when he designed the house. He chose to build on top of the island and it was an easy walk down to lower Capri. He had even thought of an arbour for Vaila, where she loved to sit and look out over the deep blue sea. Soon a vine would enclose the open lattice roof. Already it was climbing steadily upwards, winding around the stone pillars. Orange, lemon and lime trees had been planted at the back and on each side. Vaila's hand followed the outline of the Nordic design that was carved on the back of the stone seat. Tony had the pattern faithfully copied from the treasure found by May and herself when children. Her delight knew no bounds when the stonemason had delivered the seat on their first wedding anniversary.

Tony's father had the same design copied on two enormous plant pots. They stood on either side of the long, stone seat. Vaila enjoyed talking to him, and when

Tony was away sailing, they spent many hours together. Soon she became adept with the language, due to his patient teaching and her shopping expeditions. It was fun to impress Tony with her rapid progress.

Their anniversary was one of the highlights on the island. Always eager for a celebration in their midst, the residents, who had already taken Vaila and her family to their hearts, showed their feelings in many ways. "I love it here, Tony," said Vaila. "Thank you for arranging to bring my parents and Aggie out. It was such a surprise after our recent visit home. You made a hit with Aggie. Why she even eats pasta now. Your Dad loves it when she visits and makes bannocks in the kitchen." Even Maria their cook, seemed mesmerized by Aggie. "I wonder how she will take to the evening feast. Smorgasbord-type eating is unheard of in her way of life."

Tony laughed at these words. "Aggie is more adaptable than you think, darling. I have a great admiration for her philosophy of life. Even when I took her up to see where the pirate Barbarossa threw his victims down the cliff, her only comment was, 'I feel sorry for the donkeys that have to carry us all the way up to the top.'"

Vaila went into fits of laughter, saying, "Remember when you took me? I felt sorry for the donkey and walked along beside it, with the result that it was very frisky and nearly tossed me over the cliff when I finally got on its back."

"Nearly another victim for Barbarossa," said Tony, at the same time hugging Vaila very close to him. "Let's go for a swim in the Blue Grotto, darling. I know how much you love it."

"I bet you'll never get Aggie there," said Vaila. "Why she has such mistrust about the cave I'll never know." Vaila loved helping to row out to the Blue Grotto. They passed the Farangoli Rocks, so different to the smooth rocks of her own country. "I'd hate to be shipwrecked on this coastline," said Vaila. "These rocks are covered with sharp stone needles."

"It could be a protection for the island," replied Tony. "Enough talking, we are near the cave."

To get into the cave one had to lie down in the bottom of the boat. Chains were attached to the walls, and as the wave came surging in Tony pulled on a chain and magic surrounded them as the boat entered the cavern.

Vaila never forgot her first visit to the cave with Tony. As they entered, a shaft of light from above gave the place an ethereal glow. The water was of the deepest blue colour.

Tony dived in and his body seemed to turn to silver. Never in her life had Vaila witnessed such a phenomenon. To swim in the cave was sheer delight as the water was cool and clear.

Tony said the blue of the Grotto matched her eyes, but he also warned her never to come here and swim alone. It was the only restriction that Tony placed on his beloved wife's life on Capri. As he explained to Vaila, deep caverns still existed beneath the water which were yet to be explored, and at high tide the currents were very strong and dangerous.

The same procedure was followed when coming out of the Grotto, but in reverse. Vaila watched as Tony hauled on the chain and, as the wave receded, gave a mighty pull and the boat cleared the low entrance.

The island had one nightclub named the 'Heidi Gei Gei'. Vaila loved to go there when Tony was at home. The Italian dancing was exciting, and so different to her own island music. Tony was amazed at how easily Vaila took to the steps and rhythm of the dances. "You might have been born and brought up in Italy," he would say, at the same time jealously guarding her from the many requests she received to dance with his friends.

When Tony heard about the baby, he was ecstatic. "Let's announce it tonight at the party. After all, everyone will be there, darling. I hope it's a girl just like you." His voice was emotional as he held Vaila in his arms.

"Mother guessed, Tony. She said that she knew straightaway when we met them off the boat. With

Aggie there was no chance of keeping it a secret. Aggie will come over for the birth, it's all been arranged. Already she has decided we are having a boy, and his name's to be Antonio Jnr. If it is a boy, he will be the third generation of males to be called Antonio."

Tony explained, "Vaila, it is an Italian custom that if our baby is a boy he will be called 'Nino' during his childhood. He will make the decision himself to revert back to Antonio, should he wish."

"That sounds good to me, Tony, darling. This could save having a confusion of three Antonios in the family."

"You have an amazing family, Vaila," said Tony, "and I know you will be in good hands. Aggie is a special person. Even I'm beginning to believe she knows just about everything, even to the running of my ship." At these words they were both convulsed with laughter.

The party was a night to remember, after the family gathered for pre-dinner drinks. It was apparent that the whole island had been invited for the evening.

Aggie's comment was, "Now I know why you have smorgasbords in Capri."

Vaila wore a large cameo brooch, a present from Tony. She was amazed at the unusual design it depicted of the 'Three Graces'. "Where did you find it, Tony? It's beautiful. I shall wear it at my portrait sitting next week."

"I had it made especially for you in Pompeii," said Tony. "I only hope this well-known portrait painter will do justice to the most beautiful woman in the world, my wife." His love for Vaila seemed to increase as the days went by. He was delighted that the gifts he gave her brought so much pleasure.

The brooch was greatly admired by everyone, but Vaila's eyes would always look at the third finger on her left hand where the gold band showed the world of their love for each other.

Chapter 7

TIME PASSED QUICKLY ON THE ISLAND. Vaila was soon adept at speaking the language and loved to wander down to the Piccola Marina where the womenfolk shared the island washday. An enormous wooden tub stood in the middle of the square. What fun it was. The women chatted away while they washed their clothes and then piled them into a straw basket and took them home for drying.

"You have bambino soon now, Vaila," they would chorus. "Captain Antonio will want a boy," was another remark.

They were intrigued at the fine shawl she was knitting; also curious to see the knitting belt she wore around her waist. Vaila could knit and talk at the same time. With the right-hand needle firmly wedged in the Shetland belt it was incredible the speed she could attain.

The needles flashed in the sunshine and the intricate design was formed without even reading a pattern. Vaila showed them how the large shawl could easily slip through a gold wedding ring when it was finished.

"Please teach us, Vaila," they would say.

"Of course I will," Vaila replied, adding, "and you can teach me your lovely embroidery." Already she had received many hand-stitched baby clothes, and marvelled at the skill of these Italian women.

Carlos, the local boatman, was a good friend to Tony and was held in high esteem by everyone. It was rumoured that he had the gift of seeing into the future and, being an eligible bachelor, was very popular with the girls. His boat was called the *Blue Grotto*, and he made regular tourist trips to the well-known attraction.

On one of those sightseeing trips, Nan, an American visitor, started to haggle over the cost after she purchased the ticket. According to Mara, a local girl who was in the boat at the time, Carlos threatened to tip the boat over as he felt his prices were fair. Also, he prided himself on being a well-informed operator. Vaila was aghast as Mara related this story to her. "What happened?" asked Vaila.

Mara replied, "Instead of going to the Blue Grotto, Carlos returned to Capri, at the same time saying to Nan, 'You will leave the island three days from now.'"

Vaila knew that this was impossible as Nan was on a three-week vacation, having met and talked with her quite a few times at the piazza, where locals and visitors gathered each evening around 5 pm for a coffee or a glass of wine.

Most of the locals had a two-hour siesta every afternoon when the sun-drenched island seemed to fall into a peaceful slumber.

The atmosphere was idyllic and Vaila loved it when Tony was at home. They would walk arm-in-arm to the piazza to meet their friends and newcomers to the island. Nan was from the USA and could not understand why only one car was allowed on the island. "I sure think it's a funny custom you have," she would say in a loud, brash voice.

Tony, who was a born diplomat, would say to her, "There is no space for traffic on our narrow roads here in Capri; we all enjoy this wonderful feeling of peace." Vaila met Nan one day at the Villa San Michele and was taken aback by her dejected appearance. "What's wrong with you, Nan? Can I help in any way?" she asked.

"Nobody will speak to me on the island. Even staff at the hotel are barely courteous, it's terrible," she replied, in a rather hushed voice. "I've decided to leave tomorrow morning. My husband will join me in Naples instead of Capri," said a dejected Nan.

Vaila thought quickly. Tomorrow was the third day after which Carlos had predicted that Nan would leave the island. If only Tony was at home he would know what to do. "Let's look over the Villa San Michele," said

Vaila, for want of something else to say. "Do you know anything of the history of this place?" she asked.

"No," replied Nan, adding, "the architecture is beautiful."

"Axel Munthe was the creator of this villa. As a young physician, he decided to put his dreams, ambitions and ideas into reality through the creation of a home in Ana Capri. This later became world-renowned through the success of his book, *The Story of San Michele*," said Vaila.

"You don't say? Where did he come from? His name is not Italian." These questions poured forth from Nan.

Vaila thought, 'My strategy is working,' then said, "Axel Munthe came from Sweden, and died there at the good old age of ninety-two. He spent fifty-six years here in Capri."

"You don't say," said Nan. "Perhaps that's why you've been accepted, coming from the same place."

'I can't be bothered explaining that Shetland is not Sweden,' thought Vaila.

"It's nothing to do with that, Nan. The Islanders are easy-going people and many depend on tourists for their livelihood. Also, Carlos, although only a boatman, is held in high esteem by the local people."

"Easy going? I wouldn't think so," replied Nan, in a hostile voice. "Why, even the shopkeepers have turned against me. Anyway, I can get souvenirs cheaper in

Naples. Do you know, they wouldn't let me buy the miniature Capri bells? They said the bells had to be given to you by someone on the island. Ridiculous, I think. They can keep their bells for all I care."

Vaila remembered when Carlos had given her three tiny Capri bells, saying at the same time, "You are one of us." She had often pondered over his words, but the history of The Villa San Michele had made her think. Attempting to get Nan off her high horse, she went on, "Axel Munthe shared his love of music with his Swedish Queen, Victoria, who lived on Capri for health reasons for long periods at a time. They also created a sanctuary for migrating birds on Barbarossa Mountain, and both agreed that to bird lovers Capri is like a symphony of sounds." Vaila could see that Nan was impressed, especially when the bird sanctuary was mentioned.

"My husband is an ornithologist," said Nan. "He would have loved to see and hear the birds. But there are other places just as nice, I guess. On that trip to the Blue Grotto, the boatman had such a short fuse. What a fuss about discussing the price. The cheek of him refusing to take us! How dare he!" said Nan, continuing her tirade against Carlos.

Vaila realised that Nan would never change her outlook on life. Despite being a wealthy woman she was obviously out to save every cent. "Carlos would never overcharge you. He is too proud of this island and was deeply hurt that you would think such a thing. Perhaps you could put it right?"

"Never." Nan said in a scandalised voice, adding, "Me, apologise to a common boatman? That will be the day. I've no intention of leaving tomorrow. The nerve of him."

"See you at the piazza later on," said Vaila, as they bade each other goodbye. Vaila felt sorry for Nan, who had so much in life to make her happy. Unfortunately, her greed for bargains had made her many enemies on the island.

The next morning as Vaila walked down to the Piccola Marina, she saw a lone figure trudging along the narrow road, pushing an enormous piece of luggage on wheels. "Whatever are you doing, Nan?" Vaila called out.

"It's impossible to stay on this island a moment longer," said Nan becoming hysterical.

"I'm leaving right now to catch the 10 o'clock boat to Naples. The atmosphere at the hotel is unbearable. There is something going on that I don't understand. Why, they wouldn't even help me with my luggage. So much for Italian hospitality." Nan's lip began to tremble as she uttered these last few words.

Nan's being so upset while on Capri distressed Vaila greatly, and she tried to comfort her by saying, "I'll walk with you to the boat." All she could think of was 'This is... the third day,' as Carlos had prophesied.

Nan for once said, "Thanks, it's kind of you," but spoiled it by adding, "I don't know how you can stay here."

There was the usual hustle and bustle at the marina. Fresh fish and fruit were being loaded aboard the ferry. The island supplies had been unloaded and the crates were piled up on the jetty. Tourists stood around with their cameras at the ready; there was so much to be captured on film.

Carlos called out to Vaila, "I've brought the crate from Naples, and they have done a great job for you."

"Thank you, Carlos. Can it be brought up to the house today?" She felt an inward excitement, but realised she must see Nan on board the ferry first. Vaila noticed that as Nan walked up the gangway she was met with a stony silence. Her luggage had already been taken on board by one of the crew. Without even a wave, Nan disappeared into the crowded ferry and, sure enough, voices started up again with the usual Italian chatter. 'I'd never imagined that this could happen, and I must speak to Carlos about the mystery of Nan's forced banishment from the island,' thought Vaila.

As Vaila walked towards the crates wondering which one was hers, she saw tourists, obviously entranced by the drowsy Caprians, seated in front of the marina. Even the click of cameras could not budge the Caprians, as they sat meditating over the past adventures of their lives and what would be on the menu for lunch that day.

Carlos, who was by this time busy getting the donkeys ready for the daily pilgrimage to Barbarossa, called out, "See you late afternoon, Vaila, after my trip to the Blue Grotto."

"Thank you," Vaila replied, thinking how lovely the nosegays of fresh flowers looked tied to the old straw hats on the heads of the donkeys. Roses and honeysuckle grew in profusion on the island, as did lithospermum that grew out of the rocks in a wonderful deep blue colour.

Rosina, the oldest donkey, stood in her dainty black shoes with her head bent and drooping ears, looking as though she were deep in thought. Her nosegay was always extra special, made with her age and loyal service in mind. Impulsively, Vaila went forward and gave Rosina a pat. Tony was extremely fond of this donkey. He had ridden her all the time as a young boy.

Climbing the 777 steps up to Ana Capri was quite a feat. Rosina now only led the way. Alongside her walked Carlos's nephew, lightly holding on to the bridle.

Ropes were loosened and the usual farewell cries could be heard as the ferry, bound for Naples, left the pier amid much noise and chattering from the passengers and the people left behind on the marina. It was hard to imagine that this was a daily occurrence. It was more like an annual event.

Vaila gave an inward chuckle as Rosinella came rushing down the marina with the usual basket of fish on her head shouting, "Stop, stop, you must take my fish to Naples for the market!" Gesticulating with her hands, it was a miracle that the basket didn't topple off her head.

Then the usual fun started. "No, no, you are too late, Rosinella. Every day is the same with you, always late," said one of the employees of the ferry service.

"You're like Timberio, I'll spit on you," said Rosinella, as she spat on the ground. At the same time, Carlos was lifting the basket of fish on to the jetty where a boat would take it out to the ferry.

The mention of Timberio brought Vaila's mind back to the crate sitting on the marina. Not knowing the local legend, she had managed to get a very old marble bust of the Emperor Tiberius (known as Timberio to the locals) while browsing through the markets in Naples. As it was in bad condition she was advised to have it restored by a well-known craftsman in Naples. Tiberius had spent the last eleven years of his life on Capri, and was generally hated by the Islanders. Even to this day his name is used in a derogatory manner. Some of the stories told about the Emperor were vile. According to legend, he would come through a subterranean passage in the Blue Grotto, to play with boys and girls before strangling them.

Tony disbelieved these stories and felt that the Emperor had been grossly misjudged. He could quote many instances in Tiberius's favour. Vaila was delighted when she acquired the marble bust that was supposed to have been found in the Blue Grotto. It was to be a birthday surprise for Tony, who was due home in a few days.

Vaila was deeply interested in the welfare of the people on Capri, and speaking the language made relations easier. Vaila and Tony's baby son gurgled with delight when she wheeled the pushchair down the winding road to lower Capri. He was a general favourite with his blue eyes and curly black hair, and seemed to thrive on all the loving exclamations and attention he received from the Islanders. Already he knew his father's launch and would gesticulate and become very excited when he heard the three blasts on the hooter as the craft approached the Piccola Marina.

Tony's father, Antonio, was devoted to his grandson. "Vaila," he would say, "why, he's even smarter than his father was."

Vaila would laugh, "You spoil us all, Padrè. I'm glad you like my portrait. It's nearly finished, and I can only hope that Tony likes it. Without the help of Carlotta, and yourself, I'd never have found the time to sit all those hours. I don't want Tony to see it until it is finished and hanging on the wall."

"It's *bello*, my daughter, he will be delighted."

Chapter 8

Tony came home unexpectedly a few days ahead of his scheduled time. Vaila heard the three blasts that announced his arrival. Carlotta, baby Nino's nursemaid, was startled when Vaila picked Nino up and ran down to the harbour to meet Tony.

There was the usual captivating excitement going on at the Piccola Marina.

"Nino, our bambino," could be heard above all the chatter as Vaila pushed her way forward to greet her husband who had disembarked. Willing hands helped Tony who was carrying a holdall and his usual quota of parcels.

"Hello, young man," said Tony, kissing his wife, before he hoisted the baby on to his shoulders. The crowd loved this gesture and although it was time for the usual evening drink and chat, they seemed reluctant to leave. Carlos carried their bags up to Ana Capri.

Vaila had so much to tell Tony, but she was curious to hear about her friends and relatives. "Did you see Elizabeth and Hamish when you were in Aberdeen? It was lovely that Mum and Dad came down from

Shetland. Imagine Aggie making the trip! You've sure made a hit with her."

"Yes, they all send their love and can't wait for the next visit to see you and this bundle of mischief."

Carlos called out, "He's a strong bambino," as Tony's cap was pulled off by the now chortling baby, and caught by Carlos.

"Good catch, Carlos. Lucky it didn't go over the cliff," said Tony. "This road is not meant for fun and games, young man," Tony admonished his son.

They all burst out laughing at this show of chastisement. "The Farangoli Rocks look forbidding today, despite the blue sky and sunshine," said Vaila. "That's what I love about walking up this road. The ever-changing scenery, the same, but different."

They saw Carlotta anxiously waiting on her charge as they drew near the house. Knowing that Vaila was excited and wanting to show Tony his birthday present, she called out, "Come to Carlotta, my bambino, your milk and biscuits are ready."

Tony reluctantly handed over his son, who went happily to Carlotta at the mention of food.

"Come into the garden, Tony, I want to show you something."

"Thanks, Carlos. Oh, by the way, I managed to get those boat parts for you. They will be delivered to you tomorrow. I must go and see what Vaila has done to the garden. I'll catch up with you tomorrow sometime." They waved Carlos off. "Sorry darling, but Carlos is a good friend to us all. Now, let's go and see your latest handiwork."

Vaila took his hand and they walked together towards her favourite part of the garden. The stone seating looked superb against the deep green of the olive trees. The Nordic carving on the back combined with the Roman designed terrazzo pathways. It could have been designed for Tiberius himself.

There he was, the bust was placed on a marble pedestal and Tiberius seemed to complete the scene. Tony rushed forward saying, "It's marvellous. Where did you get it?"

"It took me time and of course a lot of luck at the markets, to find it," said Vaila. "I believe it was originally found in the Blue Grotto cave. I had it restored to its former glory. I only hope our friend Rosinella, doesn't spit on it. The Emperor Tiberius is certainly not popular here in Capri."

"A lot of the stories are fabrications, darling. Somehow the truth gets distorted as the years go by. Anyway, Tiberius looks good to me. How you found him is a mystery."

"Nicolena, one of my circle of friends, told me a story about Tiberius. A local fisherman wanting to please the always-disgruntled Emperor, decided to take the

Emperor's favourite spiked fish from his catch and present it to him in person. He climbed up the steep cliff, carrying his gift, no mean feat for any man. Tiberius believed that his safety was secure, as nobody had ever been able to climb that steep cliff before. On the fish being presented to a furious Tiberius, who now knew that his safety had been breached, a signal was given to the guard, who rubbed the fish into the fisherman's face and his body was thrown over the cliff that he had so perseveringly climbed. No wonder he is hated, Tony."

"Yes, I was brought up on these stories. Nicolena is a talented storyteller. Having been an English teacher at the local school, she always had a captive audience. Now that she's in her eighties, her tales are somewhat embellished."

"Your father loves his coin, 'The Tribute Penny.' It looks genuine to me. He told me that it was referred to in the Bible in Matthew 22:19 and Mark 12:15, and is popularly thought to be a silver Denarius coin of Tiberius. Also the town of Tiberius, on the western shore of the Sea of Galilee, was named in Tiberius's honour by Herod Antipas."

"Glad to hear that Dad has something different to say about my birthday present. The Emperor has been greatly maligned on this island. Tiberius's downfall was not his abuse of power but his refusal to use it. His withdrawn nature, especially in comparison with

Augustus's openness, made Tiberius a figure that was greatly disliked."

Vaila hugged Tony saying, "I'm so pleased that you like your present, darling. I think that Tiberius has found his niche here in our garden. Now, let's go indoors, I've got another surprise for you."

"Just being home with you and our son makes my life complete." With one last look at his gift, Tony took Vaila's hand as they walked towards the house.

"I wonder how Aggie will react to the Emperor Tiberius being in our garden. She is so like the Caprians in her outlook and feelings towards him."

"She'll get over it darling, it can't be any worse than your Shetland folklore superstitions. I love the style in which the stonemason carved the name of our house, 'Vaila's Capri', above the door, especially the Denarius coin depicting Tiberius, your beloved Viking boat following the Nordic design, plus the Caprian flowers and fruit, all intertwined through the name."

"Your father and I spent many hours together planning and drawing it. Here we are." Vaila pulled Tony inside the front door, at the same time anxiously scanning his face.

There on the wall, facing the front door hung the portrait. Tony gave a gasp, saying, "It's perfect, my darling! Our friend has certainly excelled himself." Vaila looked beautiful. The artist had caught her whimsical expression. Tony had insisted she wore the pale blue Shetland dress with the deep collar. "My first vision of you captured my heart forever. That night at dinner aboard the *Capri* sealed my fate," he would laughingly tell her over and over again. "Now I have you in oils. That cameo brooch depicting the 'Three Graces' was a perfect choice."

"What about my ring? It took a few sittings before Giuseppe was satisfied that my hand was in the right position."

"It matches the blue in your eyes, darling. That gold frame is a winner."

"Your father helped me to decide on the framing, along with Giuseppe, of course."

"Sounds like you were all kept pretty busy while I was away."

"I've still lots for you to do here," said Vaila. "Our son needs a swing in the garden, plus a gate at the top of the stairs."

"Now you're beginning to sound like Aggie. I must think about longer voyages in the future," quipped Tony. "I think I hear our offspring kicking up a fuss in the kitchen. Let's go and see what's going on."

"He probably wants to feed the dog. He is passionately attached to Barbarossa. Carlotta and I have this constant battle with him." Barbarossa was Tony's old Labrador.

"Now I know why Barbarossa is putting on so much weight," laughed Tony. "What's going on here young man?" Tony spoke in a stern voice to his son.

"*Canè, canè*," was the reply. At the same time he was trying to entice the dog to share his biscuit.

"Come and I'll show you where Barbarossa eats," said Tony, as he lifted up the lovable but determined Nino.

Vaila took this opportunity to discuss the menu for that night's dinner with Maria. The housekeeper, Rosina, with her quick Caprian mind, had prepared most things that morning and would be returning early evening to serve an 8 o' clock meal.

"Tony's padrè loves to come here for dinner, Vaila. You've made him so happy since you married his son. He will enjoy seeing his nephew, Atteo and wife, Margherita from Naples. I've picked the flowers for the centrepiece on the table. There's lots of blue to match your eyes," laughed Maria.

"Sometimes I wish that I'd been born with your brown eyes, Maria."

"Oh no! We all love your eyes, and the bambino's."

"I hope Tony can convince our son that dogs don't eat with us," said Vaila. "We'll walk down to the Piccola Marina for the usual evening coffee. Tony loves to meet all his friends there."

"Doesn't the marina look lovely?" asked Vaila, as they walked hand-in-hand down the winding road. "This is my favourite time of the day. Even without a watch I can tell it's around five. The birds are flying home and most of the Islanders make for a coffee and chat at the Piccola Marina."

"Put it down to an old Italian custom, darling, siesta in the afternoon, then meeting up with friends. Just look at you, pretty as a picture, in your long, colourful dress."

"That's what I love here; people are not frightened to wear bright colours. Men at home are conservative and shy away from anything that isn't traditional. Look, they've painted the wall of the café a pale pink. Along with that soft blue and gold border it looks spectacular. The glossy green leaves of the olive trees, planted in tubs around the square, seem to take on a different colour as the sun goes down."

"All I can see, darling, are full tables, and we do have to find one for Atteo and Margherita when they arrive."

"Hi, Tony, nice to have you back. Why don't you come over and join us?" said one of his friends.

"Sorry, we're meeting up with the family from Naples. They should be here shortly. We must see Carlos first and find a table. Thanks all the same," Tony replied.

Vaila felt elated to have her husband by her side and

his popularity was evident at the numerous invitations given as they walked past. "Which country does that Prince come from? He's such a friendly person. I adore his red trousers and white Afghan dog."

"Not too friendly, I hope," laughed Tony. "There are so many titled people from the Balkan countries around these days, it's hard to keep up with them all."

Clutching Tony's arm, Vaila whispered, "Look, there's Phyllis Calvert and Michael Rennie. They're my favourite film stars. I wonder if the film is finished yet."

"You might get a part in it. Imagine seeing Vaila De Marco up on the screen in 'The Golden Madonna'. We've enjoyed the drama of film-making and the free coffee. In the past when filming was going on here, I often got a few lira as an extra, just for sitting here at one of the tables. It was usually with Carlos."

"There's Carlos over there," said Vaila. "He's managed to get a table for us right on the edge where we can see Atteo's boat arriving."

Carlos rose to greet them, saying, "High tide tomorrow. I must see that all the boats are securely tied up."

"Thanks for reserving the table, Carlos. We seem to have a lot of tourists tonight," remarked Tony.

"I'm dying for a coffee and one of the marina's famous almond biscuits," chimed in Vaila. Just then the waiter arrived with two cups of coffee and biscuits.

"There you are, Vaila, how's that for service?" asked a beaming Tony.

"We always look after our regular customers," the smiling waiter replied.

Vaila was still intrigued with the small coffee cups that had a built-in filter, and were filled with the marina's special blend of ground coffee. Boiling water was poured over the filter and it was allowed to drip into the cup. This was savoured by the customers who enjoyed the fresh, black coffee. Despite the hustle and bustle all around them, they obviously enjoyed this leisurely hour or so.

"Carlos, how long will the film stars be here?" asked Vaila.

"Two more days, I think. My boat has been hired for the film, and myself, of course. They are easy people to get on with."

"Not like Nan. You must tell Tony what happened, and why."

"Best forgotten, Vaila. The island has no time for her type. I believe the film stars are visiting the Heidi Gei Gei tonight," Carlos went on, obviously not wanting to discuss the incident about Nan any further. "I'll go down shortly and meet Atteo and Margherita and will bring them back for a drink."

"Oh Tony, can we go there tonight after dinner?"

"We'll have guests, darling. Let's wait and see how

Atteo and Margherita feel about it. They may not be film-struck. Meantime, I must discuss the boat situation with Carlos."

"Moorings will have to be secured on Atteo's boat tonight, Carlos. High tide around these parts can cause a bit of trouble. Thanks for seeing to mine."

"I hope we manage the filming at the Farangoli Rocks tomorrow," said Carlos. "It can be tricky with a heavy swell."

"Nobody knows the coastline better than you, Carlos, that's for sure."

"Here's the *Amare Nave* coming," Vaila called out, rising at the same time. "Carlos, I'll go down to the marina to meet them, don't go away."

"She's probably gone to coax Margherita and Atteo to visit the Heidi Gei Gei after dinner tonight," chuckled Tony.

"I'm amazed at how easily Vaila has adapted to our island way of life," said Carlos. "She told me she has feelings of having been here before."

"Being an archaeologist and always delving into the past has a lot to do with it. Heavens, look at the gear they're unloading for an evening's stay!" exclaimed Tony.

"Probably presents for the bambino and wine from your uncle's vineyard. The finest red wine I've ever tasted. Your family never forget me, Tony."

"You're part of our lives Carlos, and everyone considers you one of the family."

Margherita and Vaila arrived pushing a shopping carrier. "Atteo will be here shortly. I believe we have to doubly secure the boat," said Margherita.

Tony fondly kissed his cousin's wife, saying, "I'm off to give him a hand."

Carlos jumped up, "I'll go with you."

"There's wine for you in the boat, Carlos. We all know how much you enjoy our Naples red, plus the family are grateful for your help in the vineyard when we're busy," said a slightly breathless Margherita.

"Thanks, I'll deliver the wine up to Ana Capri tomorrow. Have a good dinner. Here's your coffee coming now."

"Just what I need," remarked Margherita, as the two girls sat down. "I've always loved the Piccola Marina." Because they were well known on the island, there were many acknowledgements from the people. Like Vaila, Margherita wore a stunning outfit that drew many admiring glances as they sat at the table drinking their coffee.

"I think it might be fun to go to the Heidi Gei Gei tonight, Vaila. The menfolk will take a bit of shifting. Atteo loves talking to his uncle and Tony. Anyway, we'll see what happens. Here they come."

Atteo bent down to kiss Vaila, saying, "I believe you've created quite a stir on the island."

"Have I?" queried Vaila. "In what way?"

Margherita interrupted, "Nothing but silly island superstition, it's not worth bothering about."

At that moment some friends came over and the conversation was interrupted. "We're hoping to visit the Heidi Gei Gei later on tonight," one of them said. "The girls are hoping to dance with the famous Michael Rennie. Are you going?"

Tony hurriedly answered, "That depends on our visitors and the time factor."

"We'll make it," chorused Vaila and Margherita.

As the four of them walked in a leisurely manner up to Ana Capri, Vaila mused over Atteo's words, but decided to question him later. She spoke, "I love to hear the waves hitting onto the rocks below. Tonight they're giving out a different melody, don't you think?" asked Vaila.

"I can't say I've heard melodies. Why are they so different tonight?" replied Margherita.

"When the tide is higher the sound can change dramatically."

"You're a bit of a dreamer, Vaila," said Tony. "Here we are, nearly home, these parcels get heavier all the time. Let's show our guests our new garden. I'll switch on the floodlights, just stay here."

Atteo and Margherita gasped in amazement as the garden lit up. "Now I know why the Islanders are annoyed," said Atteo.

"Why, what's wrong with it?" queried Vaila.

"The Emperor Tiberius is hated by most of the people, and here you have him on a pedestal overlooking where they live. Rosinella got to hear about it through her cousin who is one of your gardeners here."

"Absolute rubbish," declared Tony. "We mustn't be ruled by tales. Tiberius stays where he is."

"What have I done?" cried Vaila, in a tearful voice.

"This is your home and garden. The whole thing is preposterous." Margherita glared at her husband, as she uttered these words.

Tony put his arm around his wife, saying, "I love my present, darling. Let's go into the house and have dinner. I know what will cheer you up, we'll go to the Heidi Gei Gei afterwards."

At these words, Vaila visibly brightened. "We'd love that. Wouldn't we Margherita?"

As they all entered the hall, Margherita exclaimed with delight at Vaila's portrait.

"It's beautiful, Vaila. Don't you think so, Atteo? The artist has done a super job."

"If I can get a word in," replied Atteo. "It's superb, worthy of a showing at the gallery in Rome."

"It stays here," laughed Tony. "Let's make for the

dining room, that's if we intend going to that film star nightclub tonight."

"I must see your son and heir first, Tony," replied Margherita. The two girls then hurried away to the nursery.

"I don't think I'll ever understand women," said Tony, shaking his head. "One minute they are rushing to get out …"

"Join the gang," butted in Atteo, "I've been married longer than you and I'm still confused."

"Anyway, let's have a drink. What'll it be, whisky or brandy?" As they sat chatting, Rosina appeared looking anxious. Tony spoke to her, "What's wrong Rosina? It's about the dinner, I suppose. I'll give Vaila and Margherita a shout. We can't have Maria's excellent cooking spoiled."

At that moment Vaila and Margherita appeared in the doorway. "Just in time," said Tony. "Let's enjoy our meal. Oh, in case I forget, Dad sends his apologies. He's a bit tired."

"I see you have a nautical influence in here," remarked Margherita. "I love that painting of your ship, Tony, especially with Naples in the background."

"That came out of my parent's home and Vaila wanted it in here," said Tony, looking fondly at his wife.

They ate the meal, which was a delicious seafood

smorgasbord. "That was most enjoyable," said Margherita.

"Let's leave the men to their coffee while we go upstairs," said Vaila. "I must see Rosina before we go, as she is staying overnight."

Chapter 9

T HE NIGHTCLUB WAS QUITE SMALL, with strings of subdued lighting and a background of tubs with glossy green-leafed ferns and palms that gave a welcoming atmosphere. A band of three young men, wearing deep red jackets and black trousers, was getting ready to start the evening's entertainment. "There are plenty of people here tonight," said Margherita, as they entered the nightclub. "I hope we get a table."

At that moment, the headwaiter, who was known to Tony, came forward, announcing, "Carlos has arranged a table for you over here."

"This is a table for eight," Tony replied. "There are only four of us."

"That's correct, sir. The film crew are coming tonight. Carlos recommended that you would be good company for them."

"Sly old dog, that Carlos! Always got something up his sleeve," laughed Atteo.

"Do you think the main stars will be here?" asked Vaila.

"He did say film *crew*, darling," replied Tony, with a big grin on his face.

"Let's have a coffee before they arrive," said Margherita. "I'm sure you'll want one, Vaila."

"Just what I need. Isn't the band super? I'm so glad that we came."

The menfolk ordered up drinks and the usual bottle of red wine was placed on the table. As they finished their coffee one of Tony's friends came up and asked if he could dance with Vaila.

Tony reluctantly agreed, saying, "Mario, don't show us all up with your dancing."

Vaila felt exhilarated as she was whirled around the small floor by this superb Italian dancer. "You dance like an angel," Mario said, in his delightful broken English.

"I love your dancing and music. I even get the sensation and feel the rhythm. It's not new to me. Something I can't explain." Suddenly, the band switched to a Tarantella, one of the island's favourite dances. Vaila fell into the steps immediately. The dance floor cleared and they were left alone.

Unaware of being the only couple on the floor, even when the spotlight was focussed on them, their dancing became faster and faster and the intricate steps climaxed with Vaila nearly touching the floor, part of traditional Italian dancing.

There was a spontaneous burst of cheering from the spectators as Mario, with a flourish only he could do, presented Vaila to the appreciative audience.

Slightly dazed at the response, Vaila waved her hand, saying, "Thank you, thank you. I love your dance."

Tony and the other four men stood up as Vaila approached the table.

"Thank you for allowing your wife to dance with me, Tony."

"Where did you learn the Tarantella, Vaila?" asked an excited Margherita. "It was perfect!"

"Hear, hear," chorused the company at their table, as the men sat down.

Tony gave his wife a hug, saying, "Please meet our guests, darling. This is Phyllis Calvert, Michael Rennie, Don Thompson, the cameraman, and Andy Simpson, the director."

Vaila felt at a loss for words. "It's lovely to meet you all."

"We enjoyed your dancing. We believe you're a newcomer to the island. Your husband has filled us in quite a bit," said Phyllis Calvert.

Michael Rennie, who sat next to her, said laughingly, "Hear, hear, I'm hoping for a dance, but not a Tarantella. I'm not up to that standard, I'm afraid."

From then on there was no gap in the conversation.

Vaila forgot her nervousness, and was carried away by Andy's knowledge of the local inhabitants.

"It's my job, as a film director, to learn about the local customs and people. No film can catch the interest of the audience unless there is authenticity and real life. I'm curious about …"

"Sorry to interrupt, Andy. May I have this dance, Vaila? This sounds like my style." Michael Rennie stood up and led Vaila on to the small floor area.

"You've certainly fascinated Andy. He's a most conscientious film-maker, always on the lookout for new ideas," said her partner, in his clear, English voice.

'What a nice person he is,' thought Vaila, as they danced, or rather pushed their way around the crowded floor. 'No thought of his own part as leading man, but ready to give all credit to his workmates.'

"Your friend, Margherita, is charming; we're all hoping to catch up before we leave Capri. Don is desperate to film the Blue Grotto. I believe you swim there." The music stopped and they returned to their seats.

Tony gave her an amused glance as she sat down and whispered to her, "Was he up to your expectations?"

"I don't know what you mean." Vaila was annoyed that her feelings of admiration had been so obvious.

"Now, I'm claiming Phyllis for the next dance," Tony said, and with that he led his partner off to the strains of "Santa Lucia". This favourite old tune was very popular with many people, and was still being played in the fifties.

Andy spoke from across the table, "Can we continue our conversation, Vaila? It looks like Mike, Atteo, Margherita and Don are happily talking together. I'll come over."

Vaila nodded in agreement and could hardly believe that Andy could be more engrossing in a conversation than her idol, Michael Rennie.

"I'm interested in your garden," said Andy. "The locals are greatly disturbed about you having a bust of the Emperor Tiberius there. They look on it as a bad omen. I know you are an archaeologist and study the science of man so you'll understand more about these things than I do. Apart from the Emperor, I would like to shoot a few scenes of your other artefacts. These, I believe, are worth seeing."

Vaila looked dismayed, saying, "The bust was a birthday present for my husband. Being new to Capri, I didn't realise how strong the resentment was towards Tiberius. I love the Caprians and would never dream of hurting them. My husband loves his gift, so I don't know what to do."

"Perhaps the locals will get used to the idea after a while. People get all het up over traditions." Andy went on to say, "I believe you're swimming at the Blue Grotto tomorrow morning, and filming that is a priority for me. Don reckons the scenery could be second to none. Unfortunately, we're due to work out on the Farangoli Rocks tomorrow morning. Seemingly, there is an exceptionally high tide which is a perfect setting for us."

"I would love to show you the Grotto sometime. It's my favourite place. Perhaps you could all come up to our home for coffee. Tony's father is an interesting person."

"It's a date. We still need some shots to finish, and to feel the atmosphere of your home would be ideal. Carlos has been a tower of strength to us, and got us through many problems. He suggested that Ana Capri would make an ideal spot for the film."

The conversation moved on to Africa. Vaila was delighted to learn that Andy had filmed The Great Ruins of Zimbabwe.

"Imagine finding a Shona's ring! I wish we could have filmed the dig. That would have been something." Andy said this in a most enthusiastic tone of voice.

"Our whole expedition was interesting. Finding out that the Shona people were definitely the original builders of the Great Ruins was an eye opener to the present day white people living in Africa," said Vaila.

"Was that knowledge suppressed, do you think?" questioned Andy.

"Yes, I'm pretty sure it was. It all had to do with white

supremacy. Thank God most of that nonsense is dying out these days."

"Can Phyllis and I join in this conversation? We need a cool drink first," said Tony, as they returned from the dance floor.

"Your husband is a good dancer, Vaila," said Phyllis. "Yes, I would enjoy a lime juice and soda please, Tony." Then turning to Andy, she said, "Oh, by the way, if you have any ideas of my dancing a Tarantella, forget it."

Everyone laughed, as Michael Rennie chimed in, "That goes for me, too. Dancing is not my thing."

"Looks like you may be stuck with the dancing, darling," Tony said, jokingly to his wife.

"No thanks, I've enough to do with our son and the house. I'll pass on that one."

Atteo then rose, saying, "Thanks for a lovely evening. I'm sure my wife feels the same way. We've to get back to Naples tonight."

"We're coming to see you off," said Vaila.

"Of course," said Tony. "I always enjoy the walk."

Amidst a lot of talk and banter they left their new-found friends with a promise to meet the next night, and made for the marina.

It was a perfect evening and the sound of the waves beating against the rocky shores added to their enjoyment, as they strolled along in a leisurely manner.

"Gosh, it's a high tide. I've never seen the boats riding so high in the harbour," said Vaila.

"I think we'd better cancel that swim. The Grotto can be dangerous as well as beautiful," said Tony in a determined tone of voice.

"Oh, no, we don't get a lot of time together. Let's make the most of it. After all, you've been swimming there all your life, haven't you? Besides, I've arranged with Rosina to look after everything for the two hours," pleaded Vaila.

"Look here, you two," interrupted Margherita. "Why not wait until the morning and see how the weather is?"

Tony agreed, obviously glad to escape an awkward conversation.

They enjoyed the walk home to Ana Capri. The road was winding and at each bend Vaila waved with great enthusiasm to their friend's boat as it quickly made for Naples.

"You'll be seeing Margherita again this week," laughed Tony.

"I really love her. She is a true friend and has helped me to settle here more than anyone."

"I'm beginning to get jealous, darling."

"You can't talk. The way you looked at Phyllis Calvert tonight."

"Why, you're jealous, darling, and I'm delighted."

With that remark he took Vaila into his arms and kissed her passionately. "Now do you believe me, my doubting wife? Let's get home quickly, and see that beautiful son of ours.

Chapter 10

"THE WEATHER'S SUPER THIS MORNING, DARLING. You're an old sleepy head. You're usually up before me. I've been to see your son, who is clamouring for his breakfast."

"Ok, I'll be with you in a jiffy," replied Tony, as he swung his legs over the side of the bed.

Breakfast was a jolly affair. "Come on, old fellow. That cereal is not for the dog. Your high chair is next to daddy, so behave yourself." Tony was besotted with his son, and the gurgles and chuckles all added to their pleasure.

Rosina, as usual, quietly got on with her duties and deftly took the baby away when the meal was over, the dog following faithfully behind.

"I do love you, Tony."

"What's brought all this on?" laughed her husband.

"I don't know. It just feels good us being in the boat together and on our way to our favourite spot. Darling,

I'm thinking of baby Nino, and wonder what life holds for him. Will he be a ship's captain like you, or perhaps an archaeologist like me? One thing I am looking forward to is introducing our son to the beautiful Blue Grotto, when the three of us all come here together to share its beauty."

"That's what I love about you, darling, your spontaneous love of life. Hey, we may not get into the cave today. The water looks very high."

"Let's try anyway. When we transfer into the cave boat I'll lie as flat as possible, while you pull on the chain and manoeuvre us in."

Tony dropped anchor and pulled on the small craft's mooring rope that was tied up to a buoy nearby. "Right darling, are you ready?" They then scrambled into the small boat. "By the way, your swimsuit matches the colour of your eyes." Tony said this between breaths as he pulled on the chain.

"I know. When I saw it I simply had to buy it. We're in! There's not a lot of ceiling room. This is the highest I've ever seen the water in the Grotto. Look at the colours."

Vaila stood poised at the edge of the boat. Her azure blue swimsuit seemed to meld in with the colours in the cave, and the love in Tony's eyes expressed his innermost feelings for his beloved wife. Vaila appeared to take on an ethereal appearance as she expertly dived off the gunwale into the cool, blue waters.

"Vaila! Wait!" Alarmed, Tony dived in after her. Where was she? Frantically, he swam deeper and deeper, desperately searching for his precious Vaila, but to no avail. Surfacing, he hoped that she would be there, but only the echo of his voice resounded around the walls of the cave.

Again he dived, unable to believe that Vaila was not there. 'She's hiding,' he thought, 'but where?' The subterranean tunnels lay further down in the cave, normally too deep for an off-the-boat dive. 'I need help,' he thought, 'the current is too strong.' He felt that he was being swept into one of those tunnels. 'Where did they lead too?'

A ray of hope swept over him. 'Could she be out in the open sea?' Desperate for air, he surfaced. 'I must get out of here and search. Vaila, my darling, you will be so frightened.' All these thoughts went through his head as he left the cave in a frenzy.

Sanity took over as Tony clambered aboard his boat. 'The distress signal, I need help.' Up went the rocket and Tony started the motor, having decided to sail around the Blue Grotto in search of his beloved wife.

First on the scene was Carlos. One look at Tony's face told him everything. Words were unnecessary. "I'll go around this way, you take the other. More boats are coming," said Carlos, in a cool, firm manner.

In no time at all the entire film crew arrived from the Farangoli Rocks nearby. Carlos waved them down and explained that Vaila was missing. "I'm going to fetch Tony. Here are more boats coming from the Piccola Marina. We need ropes and tackle. The cave must be searched. The Islanders know what to do."

An emphatic nod of assent came from Andy. He replied, "Just tell us what you want us to do." Andy thought to himself, 'This film really belongs to Vaila, and it must be completed.'

"Keep searching for Vaila, she may have drifted out to sea." Carlos then sped off to find Tony.

Some thirty boats scoured the region until it was dark, but to no avail. One or two boats decided to stay out, while the rest returned to the marina. The cave had been thoroughly explored. Even diving gear was used, complete with oxygen masks.

Carlos had tried to persuade Tony to return, but he was distraught. "We must find my wife, I'll never give up," were the only words he uttered.

One of the people in the boats had thoughtfully provided coffee and sandwiches for everyone. Having been notified of Vaila's disappearance, the womenfolk on Capri had all come to the rescue, even supplying a bottle of brandy as well as the food.

The local people on board one of the boats had volunteered to return to Capri to let the Islanders know that Vaila was missing. "Come on, Tony, let's have a coffee," said Carlos. When Tony shook his head dejectedly, Carlos said firmly, "We might be here all night," and held the cup, laced with brandy, to Tony's lips. He gulped it down, spluttering at the same time.

"That's a good fellow, let's make you more comfortable," Carlos said, as Tony leant back against the side of the boat. Within a few minutes, Tony was sound asleep from sheer exhaustion.

Carlos signalled to his friends that he was returning to Capri and called out, "I'll be back later."

Willing hands helped him to get Tony home, where Rosina and Tony's father were anxiously waiting. "We'll put him in the spare room," said Rosina, "he'll be all right there."

"I'll sit beside him until he wakes," said Tony's father, in a trembling voice.

"I've phoned Atteo and Margherita, they'll be here shortly. Atteo will join you in the search; Margherita will stay here in the house," said Rosina.

"Thanks, Rosina, you've been a true friend. I'm off now, the high water is subsiding. I'll see Atteo later," said Carlos.

Rosina decided to sleep on the lounge chair for the rest of the night. Somehow, she felt there was a lot of work ahead of them. I must peep in on the bambino, my darling child. How could all this be happening? She found him lying wide-awake talking to himself, "Bow-wow, Ma-ma." Rosina stifled a sob, picked him up and hugged him tightly, saying, as she tucked him up, "You'll always be safe with me, my precious child." Barbarossa, who slept on the floor at the foot of the cot, thumped his tail in agreement.

"I must make more sandwiches, but first I'll look in on Mr Tony and his father." Tony's father had drifted off in the chair and Tony appeared to be in a deep sleep. She closed the door quietly and went downstairs to the kitchen.

As Rosina finished making the sandwiches, she heard footsteps in the hall. It was Margherita. "It's us, Rosina. The door was open so we guessed you would be in the kitchen. Atteo and I came straightaway. Any news?"

Rosina went forward and hugged Margherita, shaking her head at the same time.

"Atteo will take our boat out now, and help in the search. We met some of the Islanders when we landed at the marina, so he is aware of the location. What can ..."

"I'm off," interrupted Atteo. "I just wanted to see you in safely, also find out if there had been any further news."

"Take these sandwiches, Atteo. Carlos, to my knowledge, has had nothing to eat."

"Thanks Rosina, I'll do that." He kissed Margherita and gave Rosina a swift hug, saying, "God bless," and hurried off.

"Sit down, Rosina, you look all in," said Margherita. "I'll make a cup of coffee first. I'm here to help and don't want any protests."

Rosina sank down gratefully, saying, "Thank you." She allowed Margherita to serve her a cup of coffee.

"Thank you, Margherita, that coffee was a real treat."

Margherita replied, "I've thought out a plan, Rosina, if it meets with your approval. Carlotta will be here soon, and she can look after baby Nino, while I look after Tony and Uncle Antonio. You will have enough to do with supervising the house. Better a plan than none at all."

"Sounds great," answered Rosina. "There's someone coming." She jumped up, ran towards the front door and opened it to find Carlos standing there looking white and ashen, with a look of despair and disbelief on his face. He was holding a blanketed figure in his arms.

In a trembling voice, Rosina asked her friend, "Carlos, is that Vaila?"

Nodding his head, Carlos said, "Lead me to the bedroom, but for God's sake, keep Tony out."

The outline of a figure wrapped in a blanket required no further questioning.

Margherita who had heard everything ran ahead and opened the bedroom door, while Rosina rushed to the cupboard for extra blankets and spread them out on the bed.

Carlos reverently laid Vaila down, saying, "I know you'll make her lovely." The tears were running down his cheeks. "I'll stand guard outside the door and make sure you're not disturbed. Atteo is downstairs."

"Is she really dead?" asked Rosina.

"Yes," replied Margherita. "We need to be strong for Vaila's sake. She would want to be dressed properly."

Rosina went to the wardrobe and brought out the blue dress with the knitted white collar that Tony loved so much. Rosina and Margherita worked feverishly to remove the wet blankets and clothing and then dried her pale skin. They then dressed Vaila reverently.

Fresh linen was put on the bed and Vaila's hands were folded onto her chest.

Within a short time the room was cleaned up and the wet clothing and linen put down the chute to the laundry. Margherita opened the door saying to Carlos, "You'd better get out of those wet clothes, there's a shower in the room opposite. I'll get you something dry to wear."

"Atteo will need the same," answered Carlos wearily.

"I'll see to that Carlos, don't worry." Margherita looked back into the room and saw Rosina on her knees at the side of the bed bidding her farewell to Vaila.

At that moment Tony appeared like a madman, pushing her aside as he rushed into the bedroom. Rosina, white and shaken, got up quickly as Tony tore in. They closed the door and the house was filled with a cry of anguish from Tony that was like nothing ever heard on this earth.

Tony's father came rushing in. The wails of the baby added to the unforgettable scene.

Chapter 11

Tony rushed down the back stairs like a man demented, and made for the garden. Rosina followed in hot pursuit. Somehow, Barbarossa, the dog, joined in the chase.

"Stop! Mr Tony, stop!" To Rosina's horror, he made straight for the edge of the cliff.

"You'll never get her, Tiberius. Never, never," he shouted. With that, he lifted the bust of the Emperor Tiberius and hurled it over the cliff. There was a sound like thunder as the marble bust crashed down the cliff face. "You're evil, just like the Islanders said," shrieked Tony, and made as if to jump.

The dog, like a flash, leapt on his master and knocked him to the ground, barking and yelping all at the same time. Rosina threw herself on top of Tony screaming, "Carlos, Carlos! Come, come!"

Margherita was first to appear. In the darkness, without a light, unless you knew the garden, it was hard to negotiate and find your way there quickly. Never would she forget the scene and sounds she heard.

A shaft of moonlight seemed to shine directly

on to Tony, Rosina and Barbarossa, and the whole place seemed to take on an unearthly silence, until a mighty wave buffeted the beach below. At that moment, a scream pervaded the night air, and the sound of rocks being dragged out to sea came to their ears.

Rosina was crying and pointing, "Look, Mr Tony! He's gone. Gone forever! Look, listen."

Margherita looked to where Rosina pointed, and only then saw, shining in the moon's light, that the bust of Emperor Tiberius was missing. Only the marble pillar was left, a grotesque reminder of the Islanders' most hated being.

Carlos and Atteo appeared and, without a word spoken, pulled Rosina up as she was clinging to Tony like grim death, repeating over and over again, "He's gone. He's gone."

Margherita had by this time switched on the light in the garden, and the scene became even more unreal. Pieces of shattered marble lay all around the pedestal where the bust had been wrenched off. Nothing could be heard but the lashing of the waves as they struck the rocks below.

Carlos was the first to break the silence, "Come on, Tony, let's get you inside." Atteo nodded in agreement.

Tony groggily got to his feet, helped by his two

friends. He looked at the empty pedestal pointing at the same time.

"Right, Tony, I'll finish the job. Hold on to him, Atteo." Carlos went forward and lifted the pedestal and sent it hurtling over the cliff.

Again an eerie cry echoed over the water. "That's a good job completed, Tony," said Carlos, in a satisfied voice. "Let's follow the girls into the house."

Tony seemed to calm down as his friend spoke these words, and with the support of Atteo and Carlos walked towards the house. As they reached the front door he flinched. "It's ok, we'll use the back stairs," said Atteo. Both men realised the painting of Vaila was too vivid a reminder for Tony at this moment.

Little did they know that from that time onwards, Tony would never use the front entrance again. The doctor was already there as they entered the room. He was attending to Rosina, who was in a state of shock.

"I'll put Rosina to bed," said Margherita. "Take Tony upstairs and the doctor can attend to him now."

Margherita insisted that Rosina have a brandy after she had helped her to shower and clean up. When she got her into bed, she said, "Rosina, I've decided to take the baby home with me to Naples."

"Oh, no!" exclaimed Rosina, vehemently. "That would be wrong."

Margherita was taken aback, and replied, "I only meant as a help to you, Rosina."

"Forgive me, but Mr Tony needs his son at this time. He must be made to realise that the bambino needs his love and care. Believe me, Margherita."

"Of course I do. You're quite right. I'll stay on here and arrange for my parents to look after our home and children. Atteo, I know will do the same. Dear Rosina, you and Carlos have a deep sense of knowing what is right and wrong."

Margherita then put her arms around Rosina and the two women wept.

"Whatever's wrong?" asked Margherita, as she turned around whilst Carlotta was giving the baby his breakfast.

Sobbing, Rosina blurted out, "It's Mr Tony. He walked right past the bambino, without even looking at him, with Carlos chasing after him."

"When?" queried Margherita.

"You were busy cooking the bambino's food. I found it strange that Barbarossa did not follow Mr Tony as he usually does."

"That dog seems to think that it's now his duty to look after Tony's son," replied Margherita.

Giuseppina, the daily cleaner, along with Carlotta, came into the kitchen, saying, "Let us know if there is anything special you want us to do. The whole island wants to help. Yes, my darling bambino," she said, as the baby called out, "Da-da, Bow-wow."

"Can I talk to you and Rosina, Margherita?" asked Atteo as he came into the kitchen.

"I'll see to the little one," interrupted Carlotta.

"Thanks Carlotta, there's a lot to be done and discussed," said Atteo, as he led the way to the sunroom.

"Tony's in a bad way and either Carlos or I will have to be with him all the time. We have phoned Vaila's parents who will be here tomorrow. Tony has particularly asked for Aggie, and as you both know she was very special to Vaila."

Rosina's eyes lit up at these words, "Aggie was a great favourite with us all when she stayed here. The locals loved her wisdom and knowledge. I'm sure she will be a tower of strength to us all, despite her age. Giuseppina has already started on the guest rooms."

"You're a treasure, Rosina," said Atteo. "Now, I'm not sure how you will all take this news. Tony is adamant that Vaila returns to her island home. His hatred of Tiberius will not allow him to have Vaila buried here in Capri. You know how the Islanders feel about their loved ones being with them here on the island. We may encounter some bitterness."

"How did Carlos react to this?" questioned Margherita.

"Strangely enough, Carlos agrees with Tony," answered Atteo.

"Then it's settled. If Carlos agrees, you can be assured the whole island will be in unison," voiced Rosina. "Where's Mr Tony now?"

"He's getting ready to go to Naples with Carlos. After all, he only has two days to make the final arrangements on Capri, and then he will be able to take Vaila back to the Shetland Islands on his ship. He must be very tired. I only hope that he's able to stand up to it due to lack of sleep and the all-night vigil with his beloved Vaila."

"It's a long journey to the Shetlands. Is that possible, Atteo?" queried Margherita.

Rosina blurted out, "I think I know why he wants to do this."

"Firstly, yes, it's possible, but rules and regulations must be followed," replied Atteo. "A lead lined coffin may have to be one of them, plus some other requirements. Secondly, Rosina, I believe you're quite right, Tony wants to relive the time they met on the *Capri* and have Vaila that much longer to himself."

Margherita was moved to tears, saying, "We'll help in any way possible. How do you think her parents will react tomorrow? After all, Vaila was their only child."

"Knowing Aggie, she will have prepared them to face up to this. But we must wait and see and use our skills and prayers for them all," concluded Atteo.

"I can hear the baby playing up," said Margherita leaving the room.

"Atteo," said Rosina. "It's the local custom for people to view the deceased. How do you think Mr Tony would feel about that?"

"As Tony himself is a Caprian, and Vaila was so much loved by the Islanders, I personally feel that Tony will come around to the local custom. He must remember, of course, that Vaila's parents should be the first to see their daughter and be allowed to spend time with her as they wish."

"Atteo," said Rosina, "I've placed a small bunch of Vaila's favourite island flowers in her hands, and later I noticed that Carlos had put three tiny Caprian bells in the centre of the posy. Is that all right?"

"Of course, dear Rosina," was the reply. "Tony, I think would be happy to see his beloved wife remembered in this way. He's too upset at the moment to be aware of anyone's grief other than his own."

"Will he ever be able to love little Nino again? The baby is bewildered, no mother and his father totally ignoring him. I'm frightened as to what the future may hold for him," said Margherita as she returned to the room.

Atteo put his arms around his wife, saying, "It's early days yet, darling. Carlos and I were surprised and delighted that he has made this one decision. To go to Naples and arrange the final details takes a lot of courage. Carlos has a calming effect on him, plus he's a true and loyal friend. Don't thrust the baby on him at the moment. We all know that his love for his son cannot die. I must go now and make arrangements to meet Vaila's family tomorrow."

At breakfast, Rosina excitedly exclaimed to Margherita, "Isn't it wonderful that Mr Tony wants us all to go down to the Piccola Marina and meet Vaila's parents and Aggie?"

"It's certainly a breakthrough, considering he has been upstairs sitting beside Vaila since returning from Naples. Carlos took a tray of food up to him, but believes he just drank the coffee. He seems to relate to Carlos in a distant way."

"Has he seen baby Nino yet?" queried Rosina. "That will be the test, won't it?"

"Unfortunately, he never acknowledged the baby when we passed him in the upstairs corridor," answered Margherita. "I was on my way to the kitchen. It looked as though he had just been having a shower. Despite the baby's cry of recognition, Tony simply nodded his head and hurried past."

"Only Aggie can help Tony at this time," said Rosina

in a determined voice. "Vaila told me of some of the wonderful things that her beloved Aggie did to solve problems and work out issues in her childhood and teenage years."

"Do you think she will stay here with Tony and the baby?" asked Margherita. "With Tony away at sea for long periods, it's going to be a difficult situation. Tony's father is getting more frail each day and you can't be here all the time, after all, you have a husband and family to consider. Atteo and I have discussed adopting the baby, and as you know, he would be brought up like our own child. Your faith in Aggie is wonderful, but then you know her so much better than I do."

"Margherita, we must consider Vaila's parents and how they feel about their only grandson. Tony's father now seems to live for his little grandson and the baby chortles with delight when he plays with him. Although frail, he seems to come to life when the bambino is around. There must be a solution, and I'm sure it will be solved in the good Lord's time."

The next morning after breakfast, Carlos appeared, saying, "The ferry has left Naples, they'll be here within the hour."

Margherita said in a surprised tone of voice, "I thought that they would have come in Atteo's boat."

"No," replied Carlos. "It was, I believe, their wish to travel in the ferry."

"We'd better get moving," said Rosina.

"I'll get the baby ready," said Carlotta brokenly.

Margherita could see that Carlotta was unable to cope any longer. "Dear Carlotta," she said, "why don't you take a few days off, and leave the baby in our care?"

Carlotta then burst into tears, saying, "I'll be back, thank you, thank you."

Margherita turned back to Carlos, saying, "Is Uncle Antonio coming?"

"No, I've just asked him," said Carlos. "He's with the bambino and will be here to greet Vaila's parents when they arrive. He's delighted that Tony and his grandson are going to meet them."

Nowadays they all seemed to use the back door. Margherita often wondered if the front entrance would ever be used again. Tony's father was already seated on the back porch as they all came out, it was as though he realised this was now the main entrance.

"Look, my grandson," he called out, "Carlos has arranged for your favourite donkey to take you down to meet your other grandpa, grandma and Aggie."

Margherita could hardly contain the excited baby as

he jumped and wriggled to get to his four-footed friend, who stood patiently waiting with his nosegay of island flowers on his head. Barbarossa stood by, waving his tail furiously.

Tony, meantime, stood aloof from the company. His face was impassive and he seemed devoid of any feelings whatsoever, even when Carlos placed Nino carefully on the donkey's back and held on to him as they slowly made their way down the winding road to the harbour. The baby loved the donkey and was ecstatic and kept calling out, "Da-da, Ma-ma."

Margherita kept thinking, as she and Rosina followed behind, how Vaila had loved the nosegays that adorned the donkeys, made up of roses, honeysuckle and deep blue lithospermum that grew wild everywhere. "Rosina, will you hold the baby when we reach the Piccola Marina?"

"Of course," was the reply, "but why?"

"The baby has been with you for so long and I think it would be nice for you to present him to his grandparents. Don't you agree?" said Margherita.

Rosina's face broke into a delighted smile as she immediately answered, "How kind of you, Margherita."

Chapter 12

THE PICCOLA MARINA WAS CROWDED and all the women seemed to be carrying a posy of flowers. The Caprians were there in force to welcome Vaila's family. "Bambino, bambino," they cried.

The baby, who was used to seeing them nearly every day, answered by chortling with delight. Carlos, who was obviously pleased at this reception, had to tighten his grip on the child.

Margherita glanced quickly at Tony, who seemed oblivious to what was going on around him.

The ferry drew in and Vaila's parents and Aggie stood beside the gangway, waiting for it to be lowered. There was a murmur of approval from the crowd as they raised their hands in acknowledgment to their island friends.

To their amazement, Tony was first up the gangway as it touched the ground, and could be seen embracing Vaila's mother and father. When Aggie's turn came, he almost fell into her outstretched arms.

Again the crowd murmured their acceptance of this act. Aggie to them was a special person.

Atteo, who was standing behind Aggie and Tony, signalled to Margherita that Rosina should bring the baby up. With much trepidation and misgiving Margherita went forward and spoke with Rosina.

Vaila's parents were first to come down the gangway and Rosina proudly carried the baby up to them. The grandmother, with tears in her eyes, fondly took the baby Nino and both she and her husband were overcome.

Rosina then took the baby from Vaila's mother explaining that she was taking her grandson up to Aggie. Already, the Caprians had come forward and pressed their posies into the visitors' hands. *Molto grazie*, was heard over and over again, and helped to break the tension.

Rosina walked up the gangway carrying an excited baby and handed him over to Aggie. There was a hushed silence as Aggie, without a moment's hesitation, promptly put the baby into his father's arms.

Tony looked dazed for a moment and then buried his face into his son and cried. Aggie took his arm and one could sense the feeling of relief that this simple action revealed to everyone as they walked down the gangway together.

"Da-da," could be heard clearly and, for the first time, a vestige of a smile lit up the proud father's face.

"Hasn't Carlos been wonderful, Margherita," said Rosina, "with the way he organised the local people who wanted to pay their respects to Vaila. The queue must have stretched from the back door to the village."

"I'll never forget," answered Margherita, "seeing Tony with his father and father-in-law all waiting to receive them at the door."

"What touched Mr Tony was that some of the women gave him toys for their bambino and island delicacies for the kitchen. He looked quite over-whelmed, and it was lucky that I was nearby to take them all away."

"Yes, I know," replied Margherita remembering. As she had walked down the road with the baby, they were met by a steady stream of local women, all laden with packages and flowers. Their delight on seeing the bambino knew no bounds. Baby Nino returned their effusiveness with gurgles of delight and was intrigued when one of the men gave him a small sailing boat with coloured sails. He was still clutching it in his sleep that night.

"What's going to happen?" queried Rosina. "Tony's father is getting so frail, but is determined to do his bit. I had to get a chair for him at the door because he wouldn't go inside."

"Vaila's mother and Aggie had laid out a table with cool drinks and Aggie's famous Shetland bannocks, which took pride of place for the mourners as they left the house," said Margherita.

"That would please the Caprians," said Rosina. Aggie had become famous for her own island dishes while on Capri. She had the knack of making friends easily and had become a loved figure in the village. "I wonder what she said to Mr Tony aboard the ship that seemed to change him."

"According to Atteo," replied Margherita, "when Tony asked her, 'Why has God done this to me?' she said, "God's not here for doing things for you. He's here to help you bear what comes.""

"What wisdom she has," said Rosina. "Somehow I feel that Aggie will help us all to make the right decisions."

"Rosina, how do you feel about the long sea voyage to Scotland?" asked Margherita. "According to Atteo and Carlos, Vaila's parents are more than willing to have the baby with them in Shetland."

"That's true," said Rosina, "but Aggie pointed out that Vaila's baby should be brought up with his father here in Capri. Although he is often away from home it's important that he realises he is needed here."

"I'm surprised that Aggie is not going with Tony and

the baby to Shetland for Vaila's funeral service. You've been a wonderful friend to all of us, Rosina, especially now that you're taking the long sea voyage to Scotland," said Margherita.

"There's quite a story to that," replied Rosina, explaining to Margherita how Aggie had discussed the possibility of she, Rosina, travelling with Tony to Scotland. Aggie herself had decided to stay in Capri and housekeep for Tony and his father. Vaila's parents were delighted and it was with their blessing they parted with their lifelong friend and housekeeper.

"That's wonderful," said Margherita. "Uncle Antonio, I believe, is coming to live here. He feels that he can amuse the baby and help in any way he can."

Rosina went on, "Aggie feels that my bambino knows me so well and Vaila's friends in Shetland will be thrilled to meet me. She also wants me to see Vaila's resting place, and be there to represent the Caprians, who were so loved by Vaila."

"My goodness, Rosina, you're so right about Aggie being a special person. Everyone has noticed the difference in Tony and Uncle Antonio since she arrived. Sort of a calm, reassuring presence is the only way I can explain it."

"Carlos and Atteo will travel over for the funeral. Meanwhile, Vaila's parents will leave in the next few days, as there will be a lot of arranging to be done in Shetland. I hope that I'm not seasick in Mr Tony's ship."

"Of course you won't be," answered Margherita in a reassuring tone of voice. "For goodness sake, you have been on boats most of your life. Haven't you?"

"Ye-es," replied Rosina, "but never in a large ship like Mr Tony's."

"Let's start thinking about clothes for yourself and the baby," said Margherita briskly. "Uncle Antonio has stated that you must not be put to any expense regarding clothes, etc, and has given me a large amount of money to cover costs for yourself and his grandson. I nearly forgot, there is an envelope here from the family to you with a sum of money for spending. Aggie has offered to look after the baby while we go shopping in Naples."

Rosina looked at Margherita in amazement, saying, "I don't need all this. Surely I'm only doing what is right."

"That may be so, but we all appreciate you so very much. Come on now, we have a lot to do."

Chapter 13

"LET'S READ ROSINA'S LETTER TOGETHER," said Margherita to her Uncle Antonio, as they sat together on the balcony.

"That would be good," was the reply. "My eyesight plays up and these confounded telephone calls are not long enough, plus they are hard to hear. How's my grandson? I miss him more and more each day. Where's Aggie?"

"One thing at a time," answered Margherita. "Firstly, Aggie has gone to the village." Aggie had become popular with everyone at the Piccola Marina and loved to visit there. Despite the language barrier she could make herself understood with her limited Caprian dialect. "I remember once," said Margherita, "Aggie trying to tell the locals how she made Shetland bannocks. Unfortunately, instead of the word for bannocks she used the Italian word *pesce*, which of course means fish. The Islanders were totally confused. However, Aggie's personality overcame all obstacles. Now, are you ready to hear Rosina's news?" laughed Margherita.

"Of course, of course," replied this lovable, but easily irritated man.

Margherita started to read:

...The journey to Cape Town was full of interest and you will be pleased to learn that Mr Tony simply cannot bear to lose sight of his son for a minute. While I remember Margherita, your tablets must have helped me. I've not been seasick. The crew have been wonderful to us. When your relatives came on board at Cape Town, it was a great reunion despite the tragic circumstances.

One of the ship's crew had gone ashore early that morning after we had docked and brought loads of fresh flowers to decorate the cabin where Vaila lay. The perfume and décor was lovely when your family went to pay their last farewell.

Two of the Shona tribesmen travelled from the Great Ruins of Zimbabwe to honour Vaila. Seemingly, she was held in high esteem due to her discovery of the Shona ring. Earth was brought from the ruins and according to their wishes would be buried with the coffin.

Mr Tony was very touched and spoke to them of the great honour they had bestowed on his wife. I must confess I shed a tear myself.

The bambino received many gifts from his doting

relatives, but his favourite toy at the moment is a carved Zimbabwean bird given to him by these two Shona men.

I'm sure Aberdeen must have been traumatic for Mr Tony. Although I had never met Vaila's friend, James, she had told me a lot about him. I wonder how he has coped with Vaila's death.

Vaila's friends and relatives lined the wharf when the ship eventually docked. As there was a cargo to be unloaded, we were invited to Hamish and Elizabeth's home in Aberdeen for lunch and then taken to the airport for the final journey to Shetland.

Mr Tony had to see to final details and met us at the airport. Thankfully, your husband and Carlos met Mr Tony and helped him on the final leg of the journey. Aggie, you were fondly remembered by everyone and I felt honoured to be taking your place.

The Island of Vaila was beautiful, and a wonderful resting place for our beloved Vaila. The sea encircles the island and although there are no trees, there is something magical in the atmosphere. The sky is not blue and the sun is not hot, but the sound of the waves hitting the rocky shores was reminiscent of our own island.

A cool breeze was blowing as Vaila was lowered into the ground and perhaps it was a figure of my imagination, but I smelt the perfume of oranges and *lemons waft over us for a fraction of a minute. Carlos met my startled gaze and nodded to me as though in complete agreement.*

Lovingly yours, Rosina.

As Margherita finished reading the letter, her uncle exclaimed, "Rosina and Carlos loved Vaila. Aggie arranged it all to perfection. Vaila often spoke about the perfume of oranges and lemons as she sailed into Capri, and remembered the cool breezes of the northern hemisphere."

Margherita took his hand, saying, "Vaila will always be with us." Her uncle replied, "Yes, and she will live again through her baby son, my grandson."

*Irene Mouat (2nd from the right), cousin to the author, together with ladies
from the Island of Unst, admire a fine lace shawl which was knitted
by one of the island women.*

*Showing the fineness of a Shetland shawl at the Unst Heritage Centre,
and how it can be passed through a gold wedding ring.
Photographs by John Coutts.
(Courtesy of the Ladies of the Unst Heritage Centre.)*

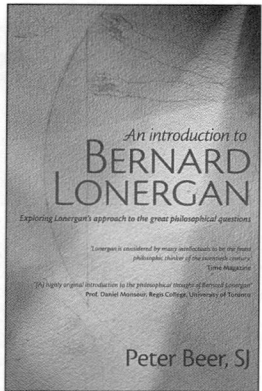

New Releases… also from Sid Harta Publishers

OTHER BEST SELLING SID HARTA TITLES CAN BE FOUND AT

http://sidharta.com.au   http://Anzac.sidharta.com

***

HAVE YOU WRITTEN A STORY?
http://publisher-guidelines.com

Best-selling titles by Kerry B. Collison

Readers are invited to visit our publishing websites at:
http://sidharta.com.au
http://publisher-guidelines.com/

Kerry B. Collison's home pages:
http://www.authorsden.com/visit/author.asp?AuthorID=2239
http://www.expat.or.id/sponsors/collison.html
email: author@sidharta.com.au

Purchase Sid Harta titles online at:
http://sidharta.com.au

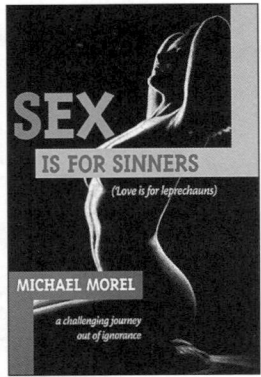